MW01129001

A MOST FATAL WAR

A TRUE STORY OF BENJAMIN CHURCH

A MOST FATAL WAR

P. GIFFORD LONGLEY

A Most Fatal War
Copyright © 2018 by P. Gifford Longley. All rights reserved.

Scripture quotations taken from the New American Standard Bible®, Copyright © 1960, 1962, 1963, 1968, 1971, 1972, 1973, 1975, 1977, 1995 by The Lockman Foundation. Used by permission.

Edited by Barbara Longley MacGregor

Independently published in the United States of America

ISBN: 9-781720-191162
1. Fiction, Biographical
2. History, United States, Colonial Period (1600-1775)

DEDICATION

King Rehoboam consulted with the elders who had served his father Solomon while he was still alive, saying, "How do you counsel me to answer this people?" Then they spoke to him, saying, "If you will be a servant to this people today, and will serve them and grant them their petition, and speak good words to them, then they will be your servants forever." But he forsook the counsel of the elders which they had given him, and consulted with the young men who grew up with him and served him.

—I Kings 12:6-8

ACKNOWLEDGEMENTS

I wish to thank my wife for her great patience with me for allowing me the time to work on this book.

I also give my sincere thanks to my editor, my cousin Barbara Longley MacGregor, for her insight, critical commentary, and for her skill. I am delighted we have done this project together and am sure our grandparents, George and Madeleine Longley, are smiling down on this collaboration.

FOREWORD

"WE LEARN FROM HISTORY THAT
WE DO NOT LEARN FROM HISTORY."
—HEGEL

Today's average American has never heard of King Philip's War. They could not tell you it was fought in New England between 1675-1676, and was finally concluded in 1678. They could not tell you who Philip was, supposing he might be some Spanish monarch. They could not tell you Philip was a Native American, that his birth name was Metacom (or Metacomet), that he was a Wampanoag, a Pokanoket Sachem, and the son of Ousamequin, whom the English called Massasoit, which means "Great Chief." They could not tell you that the war's belligerents were five tribes of Native Americans on the one side, and on the other the English settlers, aided by two more Native American tribes—nor could they name any of those tribes. They could not tell you any names of the commanders and leaders from either side. They could not tell you the reasons for the war, the outcome, the impacts on both sides of the conflict, or even the legacy that lingers to this day. Clearly, King Philip's is a forgotten war.

In the excellent book *King Philip's War – The History and Legacy of America's Forgotten Conflict[1]*, authors Eric B. Schultz and Michael J. Tougias thoughtfully explain the many aspects and facts of the war, its cause, actors, outcome, and legacy. They also point to some surprising statistics. During the whole of King Philip's War, it is estimated that eight hundred English were killed. And while that figure might seem small, it amounts to 1.5% percent of their entire estimated population of English settlers; which translates to a toll that is nearly double the rate of deaths in the American Civil War, seven times the rate of Americans killed in World War II, and nine times the rate of deaths in the American Revolution. There is little doubt that by 1678 every European settler living in New England either had a family member who had died or had an acquaintance who had been killed in the war. And if these statistics for the English settlers are not shocking enough, the Native Americans fared far worse; they incurred an estimated three thousand deaths in King Philip's War, a staggering rate of 15% of their population, ten times that of the English.

These facts, in my mind, make King Philip's a most fatal war, which makes it a war we must try and understand. I hope this book will make King Philip's War a bit better understood, and a lot less forgotten.

—P. Gifford Longley

---

[1] The Countryman Press, Woodstock, Vermont, 1999

NOTICE TO READER

I became aware of Benjamin Church when I was researching my first two books, *Captive* and *Compelled*, which were released in 2011. I was fascinated then by his character and the key role he played in King Philip's War, a conflict that had no small impact on the culture and circumstances that would lead just a half-generation later directly to the deaths of my eight-great grandparents. I was drawn to Church's attitudes, which flowed out of the earlier colonial days of peace and prosperity between the Native Americans and the Pilgrims. I saw Church as a man who wanted to return to earlier ideals, and who had a healthy disdain for attitudes of his culture that were changing all around him, changing for the worse.

I thought back then, before my books were released, that I might want to come back to Benjamin Church and create a modern retelling of his life—a life I considered to be remarkable. Hence I have now ventured and assembled this work, following in the style of my previous books: telling Church's story through the eyes of the characters who lived it, telling it "in the moment," absent perspective that comes only "after the fact," and, all-importantly, founded on historical records. In the absence of facts, I have completed the story with enough conjecture necessary to bring the characters fully back to life. The outcome is a novel in the genre of truth-based historical fiction.

The primary source of the story (Parts One, Two, and Three), comes from the *History of King Philip's War by Benjamin Church, with Introduction and Notes by Henry Martin Dexter;* published in Boston by John Wilson & Son, 1865. Dexter's book was the fourth edition of Church's work. The original was published by Benjamin's son, Thomas Church in Boston in 1716 under the title *Entertaining Passages related to Philip's War.* Benjamin died shortly after that first printing, on March 5, 1718 in Little Compton, Rhode Island; he was seventy-eight. A third edition of *Church's Philip's War,* was published in 1827, with reader notes by Mr. Samuel Gardner Drake, which I also found to be a valuable resource.

The notes in the two editions by Drake (1827), then later by Dexter (1865), are extremely helpful in understanding Church's history. These explain the geography, the location of events (Dexter's has a wonderful map—the basis for the maps in this book), the timeline and dates, the full names and biographies of characters that Church mentions only by last name, and references contemporary 17th century historical perspectives to aid in understanding some of the events. I found Dexter's notes to be particularly useful and insightful (I should say "correct") as he unravels and lends light to the stories. I am particularly impressed with Dexter's research into the Almanac, which he uses to pinpoint Church's casual references to a "full moon" or "lunar eclipse" onto a precise date. In more than a few locations, Dexter's observations sought to correct errors and inconsistencies in Church's own sequence of events, sequences that Dexter opined had been unintentionally misremembered by the elderly Benjamin Church as he assembled his work some forty years after the events had occurred. There appeared, in my opinion, to be just two instances in which the brilliant Dexter may be in error—those are the sequence of the deaths of Anawon and Tispaquin, and the role of Alderman in revealing the location of Philip. The rest of Dexter appears to me to be entirely authoritative.

As to Church's original text, the modern reader would find it very difficult to read, particularly with the then-common use of the font "f" where "s" is intended, and the archaic use or absence of punctuation. In addition to these problems of legibility, a number of Church's words and idioms have meanings foreign to today's reader. For example, "he was soon on the full career on horseback" means "he leaped onto his horse and rode hard." This collective combination of grammatical, cultural, idiomatic, and linguistic changes in the English language over three hundred years makes Church's book what it is: a work consigned largely to be forgotten.

But it should not be forgotten.

My goal in this work was to include as much of the original Church as remains reasonably comprehendible, and to update the language of the rest so that the whole of the story can be easily understood and appreciated by the modern reader. His work, after all, is a personal memoir of singular value, and provides to us a window into the workings of his mind and into the feelings and beliefs of the twin cultures that surrounded him—English and Native—cultures that were so violently at war with one another. But my goal was not to stop there with a simple paraphrase, a modern translation of Church. This book has more. It has new material to help the reader understand Church and his time, it incorporates Dexter's observations, implements his corrections and re-sequences events, it folds in bits from parallel accounts not known to Church, and it expands

Church's descriptions and conversations to make for a clearer visualization of the people, places, and events. And beyond producing a work that I believe to be in large measure historically correct, I hope that it has been rendered in a manner that the reader will find *"entertaining,"* to quote Church's own title.

In closing, I leave the reader with the words of Benjamin Church himself, who, in 1716, so artfully and plainly explained the purpose he had in preserving his own story.

—P. Gifford Longley

TO THE READER

THE subject of this following narrative, offering itself to your friendly perusal, relates to the former and later wars of New England, which I myself was not a little concerned in. For in the year 1675, that unhappy and bloody Indian war broke out in Plymouth colony, where I was then building, and beginning a plantation at a place called by the Indians "Sakonnet," and since by the English "Little Compton." I was the first Englishman that built upon that neck, which was full of Indians. My head and hands were full about settling a new plantation where nothing was brought to; no preparation of dwelling house, or out houses, or fencing made. Horses and cattle were to be provided, ground to be cleared and broken up; and the utmost caution to be used, to keep myself free from offending my Indian neighbors all round about me. While I was thus busily employed, and all my time and strength laid out in this laborious undertaking, I received a commission from the government to engage in their defense: and with my commission I received another heart, inclining me to put forth my strength in military service: and through the grace of GOD I was spirited for that work, and direction in it was renewed to me day by day. And although many of the actions that I was concerned in were very difficult and dangerous, yet myself, and those who went with me voluntarily in the service, had our lives, for the most part, wonderfully preserved, by the overruling hand of the Almighty, from first to last; which doth aloud bespeak our praises: and to declare His wonderful works is our indispensable duty. I was ever very sensible of my own littleness, and unfitness to be employed in such great services; but calling to mind that GOD is STRONG I endeavored to put all my confidence in Him, and by His almighty power was carried through every difficult action: and my desire is that His name may have the praise.

It was ever my intent, having laid myself under a solemn promise, that the many and repeated favors of GOD to myself, and those with me in the service, might be published for generations to come. And now my great age requiring my discharge from service in the militia, and to put off my armor, I am willing that the great and glorious works of Almighty GOD to us children of men, should appear to the world; and having my minutes by me, my son has taken the care and pains to collect from them the ensuing narrative of many passages relating to the former and later wars; which I have had the perusal of, and find nothing amiss as to the truth of it; and with as little reflection upon any particular person as might be, either alive or dead.

And seeing every particle of historical truth is precious; I hope the reader will pass a favorable censure upon an old soldier, telling of the many rencounters (unpleasant experiences) he has had, and yet is come off alive. It is a pleasure to remember what a great number of families, in this and the neighboring provinces in New England, did, during the war, enjoy a great measure of liberty and peace by the hazardous stations and marches of those engaged in military exercises, who were a wall unto them on this side and on that side. I desire prayers, that I may be enabled well to accomplish my spiritual warfare, and that I may be more than conqueror through *JESUS CHRIST* loving of me.

—*BENJAMIN CHURCH*

Introduction

In 1620, one-hundred-two English settlers crossed the Atlantic Ocean on board the Mayflower and came to America. Most were Pilgrims, a separatist-Christian sect, seeking freedom from the Church of England, which they saw as corrupt. They were bound for a new home and a new life in their own settlement in the English colony of Virginia.

On November 9th, they came alongside the coast of Cape Cod, and then spent the next two days trying to round it, to continue to the south. Faced with unrelenting winds and waves in the straits south of Chatham, they turned back north, rounded the northern tip of the cape, and dropped anchor off the shores of what is today Provincetown, Massachusetts. There, while they remained on board, they formed the Mayflower Compact, which established how they would govern themselves. And as they waited in the protection of that harbor, they began to talk about the possibility of staying right where God had led them. Then exploring the Plymouth Bay, they eventually decided to settle on its western shore, up against the mainland, in a place they would call Plymouth. In December, they came ashore and hastily erected shelters. In that first winter, half of them died from a variety of maladies: malnutrition, exposure, accident and disease.

When March came and the first green shoots began to emerge from the ground, an Indian walked suddenly into their camp. He spoke English, to their great shock, and introduced himself as Samoset; he was Algonquin, from Pemaquid, Maine. For years he had been traveling along the New England coast with English fisherman, and in the process, had acquired their language. Samoset told the Pilgrims that they had settled in an area that had four years earlier been occupied by the Patuxet Indians. He then explained that every single one of them, every man, woman, and child, had died of a plague; the incidence of which had led many of the neighboring tribes to stay clear of that place, believing that the land was under a curse. The Pilgrims immediately understood how they had been able to occupy a piece of wilderness that had been cleared for them, and recognized that the hand of Providence had cursed the land for their own protection—for Samoset told them also that the Native Americans in that region had reputations for their warlike behavior, and for killing Europeans.

Samoset had been living the last eight months among the Pokanoket Indians, some fifty miles to the southwest. He told them about the leader of those people, Massasoit, who was from a tribe of the Pokanokets. He also told them there was another Indian living among the Pokanoket who spoke much better English than he did, an Indian by the name of Squanto. At the conclusion of their discussion, the Pilgrims gave Samoset some gifts and he departed.

A week later, Samoset returned with Squanto, who would become the Pilgrims' point of entry into a measured relationship with the Pokanoket leader, Massasoit, then about the age of thirty-nine—"Massasoit" was a title used by the natives, which was translated as "Great Chief." In April, the Pilgrims formed a treaty with Massasoit and the two peoples began a relationship of mutual aid and assistance; in short, they would support each other in defense against the adjacent warring tribes. This had an immediate benefit to Massasoit, who was greatly concerned about his populous and imposing neighbors to the west, the Narragansetts. The Pilgrims, under the military leadership of Miles Standish, had muskets.

After the treaty had been established, Massasoit returned to his home, but Squanto remained behind with the settlers. Squanto, it turns out, was a Patuxet. Some fifteen years earlier, he had been scooped up by the English Captain George Weymouth, who had been exploring the New England coast. Weymouth took Squanto (whose full Indian name was Tisquantum) and four other Indian boys back to England where he intended to teach them English, so that they could provide him with intelligence regarding the Native Americans who occupied New England. In 1614, Squanto was returned to his home by Captain John Smith, who was then mapping the American coastline. A short time later, Captain Thomas Hunt, whose ship was part of Smith's expedition, took hold of Squanto and clapped him in irons and promptly sailed him and nineteen other boys to the Mediterranean city of Malaga, where he intended to sell them as slaves. Arab traders bought most of the young Indians and shipped them off to North Africa. But monks from a nearby monastery had heard about the deed, and were able to buy and free the rest, including Squanto. Squanto remained a while in their care, but proving himself to be resourceful, he soon found his way on board a ship to London, and then back to New England, arriving there in 1619. Returning to his village to reunite with his family and friends, he found there only skulls and bones; the plague had killed everyone. Despondent, lacking any purpose in his life, he wandered aimlessly around southeastern New England. Eventually he made his way to Massasoit's village, where he was welcomed and taken in. He had been there six months when Samoset came to tell him of the new English settlers who were occupying his former home.

Squanto saw quickly how the Pilgrims lived, how ignorant and ill equipped they were for survival in North America, how they had brought with them only English wheat, barley, and peas. Recognizing they were headed toward starvation, he became energized with new purpose. He stepped down into the shoals, stomped on a dozen eels, gathered them up in his hands and brought them up to the surprised Pilgrims, who quickly found the eels to be sweet and tasty. And as they were eating their first good meal in a while, they were no doubt reflecting on the fact that in four months of fishing, they had managed to catch only one cod fish, one fish in an area renowned for its abundance of fish ("Cape Cod"). Squanto showed the English how to build weirs in the streams, so that they could harvest hundreds of fish. He showed them how to plant corn and pumpkins to reap bounty from the rocky New England soil. He showed them how to harvest maple sap and boil it into syrup, how to identify which herbs were good for medicine, and where to find the best berries. He showed them how to stalk deer, and he showed to them how to catch beaver and treat their pelts, which would become for them a major item for trade to help them settle their debt with their European financiers. In short, his new purpose in life was to help them to save and better their own lives. And in the process, they became good friends.

In November of 1621, a year after the Pilgrim's arrival, the first ship came from England, bringing family members and new settlers, but no new supplies. Still, thankful for their survival, the Pilgrims celebrated a meal of thanksgiving, sharing with Massasoit and his people the little of what they had.

In the early years of the relationship, the two peoples held a distant respect for one another, one that was undermined by mutual distrust. To the natives, their perspective on the Europeans was tainted by stories of kidnappings, and English disrespect for native culture, possessions, and land. For the English, their perspective was overwhelmed by their belief that the natives were barbaric and godless. Attempts by Christian missionaries to convert the natives had not helped, meeting with mixed responses. A good number of natives did embrace the belief and became "Praying Indians" to their own trouble among their kin. But many others were roundly offended by the proselytization; they rejected the "English God" and the non-biblical cultural baggage and attitudes that were inextricably bound in with the Christian message.

Three years into their commerce, the tenuous relationship between the two peoples changed when Massasoit fell deathly ill, bearing symptoms that today sound like those that accompany typhus. When Edward Winslow, one of the Pilgrim leaders who would later serve as Governor, heard of it, he rushed to Massasoit's side to see if he could help. Being weak and full of fever, even blind from the disease, the great chief allowed himself to be treated. For three days, Winslow stayed at Massasoit's bedside, tending to him, giving him the medicines he had, and using all of the peculiar medical knowhow he had learned over the years, which included scraping the furry "corruption" from the Indian's swollen tongue with a knife. Remarkably, Massasoit made a full recovery, and then promptly ordered that Winslow treat all of the people in his village.

Thus began a normalized relationship, one that was properly founded by mutual respect and trust, one that would allow the Pokanokets and English to live side-by-side as good neighbors, aiding one another, and enjoying peace.

During these years, Massasoit's power and prestige increased, and he grew to rule over the nation of the other native tribes in southeast New England, which collectively came to be known as the Wampanoag. In later years, enjoying the protection of his English allies, Massasoit changed his name to Ousamequin (or Usamaquin).

* * *

But by forty years after the English first settled in Plymouth, the relationship between settlers and natives had changed. In 1655, Edward Winslow died at the age of sixty, followed just six years later by Ousamequin, who had reached the ripe old age of eighty. A new generation took over; both their sons rose to power; Wamsutta became leader of the Wampanoag peoples, and Josiah Winslow would eventually become the governor of Plymouth Colony. And in the spirit of harmony between the Pokanoket and the English, Wamsutta, changed his name to Alexander, while his younger brother, Metacom, changed his name to Philip.

Alexander was not in power for very long before a crisis arose between the peoples. In 1662, he was summoned, and then taken against his will, to Plymouth to discuss the rumors that he had been in negotiation with the Narragansetts to attack the English. At the meeting, Alexander grew suddenly and gravely ill. He left for Josiah Winslow's house to receive medical attention, trusting himself to the care of English medicine, just as his father had once before. But Alexander's illness was not the same. He was carried back to his home at Mount Hope and died there within the week.

Philip was now the leader of the Wampanoag. And Philip was convinced his brother had been poisoned.

Maps

The maps included are based upon an excellent map included in the fourth edition of *Church's Philip's War*, with an introduction by Henry Martyn Dexter, Boston, 1865.

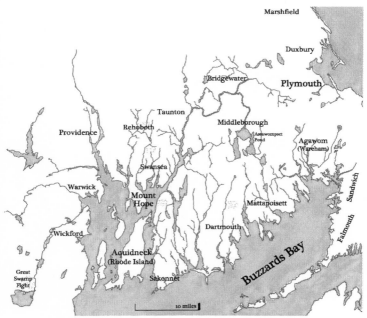

Plymouth Colony and Rhode Island, 1675

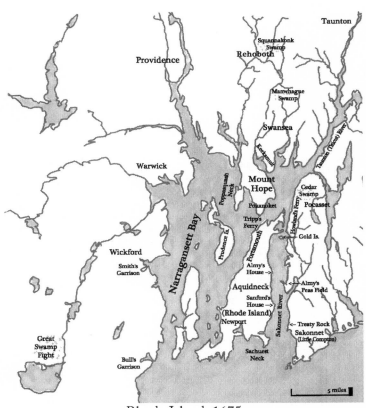

Rhode Island, 1675

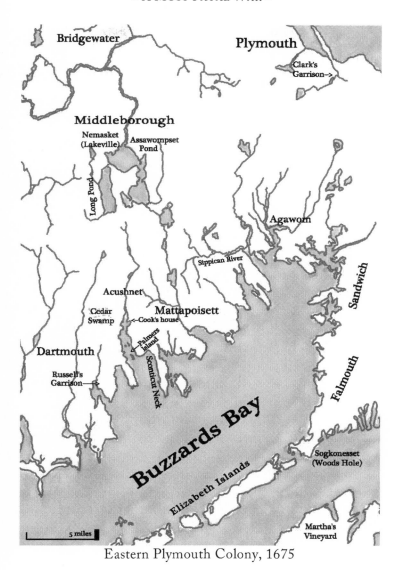

Eastern Plymouth Colony, 1675

Prologue

1

John Sassamon kept running, certain he was being followed.

Nearing the trailhead at the edge of his field, he peeked over his shoulder, back down the leafy path. No one was in sight. Still he reasoned it foolish to veer off, to return to his home; they would find him there. Instead, he pushed ahead on the trail as it skirted the edge of his pasture, leading him away from his comfort.

He glanced up into the grey overcast; it was not quite evening, his time for safe hiding. He quickened his pace, sprinting toward the bramble doorway that advanced from his field into the eastern woods, anxious to make it there unseen.

John ran from the clearing a few paces into the tree line. He stopped in the middle of the path, winded; he'd been running for miles. He lurched forward and grabbed his knees. He wished he was young again, remembering how he could run for hours, hardly breaking a sweat. He huffed out clouds of steam, trying to calm himself, holding his chest, feeling his heart pounding. He knew it. *Those days are gone.*

He closed his mouth to silence his breathing, raised his eyes, and focused on the trail, looking back across the field. He waited for the men to emerge. He swallowed hard and

33

listened. The damp in the air descended as a fine, frozen mist. It had started to snow.

Silence now smothered the woods as the tiny flakes drifted down between the bare branches, falling on the frozen leaves. If he was going to hide, to conceal his route, he had better do it now. This snow was not going to melt.

He turned again up the path, willing his aching legs farther into the forest. He quickened his pace. In a few steps he was back at full speed.

John knew these woods well. He was on the main route, well trod by native and settler bound for Middleborough and beyond to points east, to Plymouth. There were no side roads in this section and no neighbors for miles. But to the right there were narrow openings through the thickets that led down to the pond, paths that had been blazed by wildlife and hunters. He would take one of these and hide in nature's labyrinth.

The limbs overhead fell away. He slowed to a walk and stepped out into the low-lying scrub that surrounded the little lake. It was brighter there. Ahead he could see Assawompset Pond. Earlier in the day it had been glistening with new ice. But now, despite the gloom, it was yet prominent, wearing its first thin cover of white. This was a good place to hide, to get still, to wait while they passed him by on the main road.

John found a grassy spot beside the path, under the protection of a hawthorn tree, its branches tangled with a canopy of dried leaves. He flopped down and rested as the snow continued to fall.

Darkness fell quickly and the air turned colder. The snow blanketed the air, gathered on the ground, and stuck to the trees. Every movement, every tone, was silenced; the quiet was overwhelming.

And in this void of the senses, all John could do was fret. He buried his head between his knees and clenched his fists, silently repeating his conviction.

I did what I had to do.

He mulled those words again and again. He imagined the false accusations and fancied his skillful defense. And as he warred within himself, he longed to throw open his mouth and scream out the truth. But there was no one there to fairly judge; no one to hear his case. He huddled to stay warm.

Hours passed.

A stiff breeze whirled through the grass and tossed the snow sideways.

John raised his head and squinted at the sky. The moon was overhead, glowing through the thinning, fast moving clouds. It was clearing. The snowfall had stopped.

John rose stiffly to his feet and stepped forward onto the path. It had gotten very cold. He stomped his moccasins on the ground to warm his legs. He examined the area. The snow was barely an inch deep. His eyes traced forward on the trail that led down to the pond. The wide oval was aglow in white.

John felt the beauty of the place. And even as his face chilled and his body shivered, his spirit too had cooled off. He *had* done the right thing. *There is no doubt. There must be peace.* That was settled.

Now he was just a few minutes from home. *How dear it will be to go lie down and sleep!* He sighed, having vanquished his fear, ready to turn and ascend the trail back up to the main road.

John never saw his attacker. A hand grabbed his wrist from behind. A second, a burly forearm, swept over his shoulder and clamped across his chest. It squeezed up tight beneath his chin, wrenching his neck. His assailant leaned back and lifted John's feet off the ground, then flailed him left to right and back again, shaking his body like a rag-doll.

John's right hand was free. He reached up to the arm that was choking him, clawing at it. He gouged his fingernails into the skin but could not pry it off. He remembered his knife, sheathed at his belt. His fingers fumbled with the strap, freed it. Spinning the grip in his palm he took a firm hold, raised his arm, and plunged the blade downward, backwards into the thigh of his attacker.

His assailant screamed and released him, falling away. John let go of the knife and lurched forward to the ground, clutching his throat, then scrambled to his feet and stumbled forward several paces down the path.

His mind flashed. *I should run, but where?* The path split three ways: one left, one right, one down to the pond. He paused; his neck and head throbbed. He brushed his neck with the back of his wrist, and dropped his hand to examine it in the moonlight. *No blood. Good.* But still, it was killing him. He caught his breath and turned to run left.

Another man was there, in the path, standing distant.

John gasped, whirled and took two steps in the opposite direction.

A third assailant stood ahead; his arms extended like a fence.

John turned once more up the path he'd come in on. His attacker had regained his feet. The big man stepped forward, dragging one leg, huffing out a cloud of anger. He was brandishing John's own knife now in his fist.

The path to the pond was his only choice.

John eased himself backwards toward the pond, step by step, purposefully facing his three assailants as they slowly converged. He lifted the strap of his musket up over his head and neck, and swung the weapon around to the front, gripping the gun in both hands. He knew they couldn't know the weapon wasn't charged and ready to fire at them. But that wasn't why he had removed it from his back.

The men stopped.

He edged backwards, closer to the pond. He shifted the gun into one hand as he reached for the cord that held the fowl, the day's catch on his back. He raised the line up and over his head and discarded the birds to the ground.

Stepping back, John had reached the edge of the ice. He loosened his pouch and dropped it in the grass. Again he took his musket into both hands. He studied their dark faces as his fists squeezed the weapon. This was the moment.

John tossed the gun, turned, and scampered out onto the ice.

Under his feet, John felt the bending of the surface as it creaked and moaned beneath his weight. He stopped running and slid on the glassy surface, slick under the powdery snow, holding both arms out to maintain balance. He skated to a halt some thirty paces from the shore, turned, and faced them.

The three stood at the shoreline. They dared not follow. The ice was merely five days thick.

Loud cracking came all around him, radiating inward, straining, snapping, fracturing. John stretched his arms out and inched his feet farther apart, spreading out his weight. He held his breath. The groaning of the ice stopped. He stared at the men and let out a sigh of relief.

Yet with no further sound, the ice gave way. John plunged through the breach, down into the water. A shard of ice slit his throat as he fell through.

Sinking into frigid silence, John peered upward. He watched the waxing moon recede, darkened by his own blood. This was the last image he saw.

John Sassamon was dead. His body lay buried beneath the ice, vanished from view.

His assailants imagined no one else had seen it happen. But the ice could not hold its secret forever.

2

JANUARY 29, 1675

The morning sun had cleared the treetops, blaring through the frigid sky and onto the snowy surface of Assawompset pond. For a week the temperatures had been at winter lows, thickening the ice, making it safe to tread. This fact brought out the native fisherman, each conjuring the taste of savory, fresh black crappies (calico bass) sizzling on an open campfire. The group of men and boys had trudged from miles away for their mid-winter meal, traveling through the ankle deep snow, carrying their axes and fishing gear, looking for places to dig their holes. It was a father and son event.

Thirteen-year-old Wuskenin had a good idea where to find the best fish. He made his path away from the others, farther down by the western shore. Satisfied with his location, he cleared a spot to set his gear down, scuffing his boots sideways to sweep the snow away. He dropped to his knees and enlarged his clearing, pushing the last of the powder away with his forearms. Then he reached for his axe.

But before he made his first cut, he bent and blew the last of the flakes away, exposing the polished surface, opening up a crystal portal into the darkened depths of the pond. He cupped his hands round his eyes to shield the sun, squinting into the deep, spying for the fish.

The boy shot to his feet. "Noeshow!" he shouted toward the others.

His father ran to join him. The others followed, surrounding the boy, now stooped, his face ashen. They asked him what was wrong.

The boy pointed toward the clear spot in the ice and muttered, "Squi—boququo—" then covered his mouth and eyes.

Wusekenin's father got down on his knees, shielded the glare, and peered through the ice. There, he saw what his son had seen, the red and bloated head of a man, with frozen eyes gazing up at them—dead eyes. He pushed himself to his feet and addressed one of the elders, "Take the boys ashore." He turned to the other men, "We have some work to do." While the boys were being ushered away, he explained the gruesome discovery to his fellows.

The men wielded their axes and made an opening in the ice. They pulled the man up and out from the black water, then lay him there and examined him, hoping to identify him. The garb was Pokanoket, a tribe from the southwest, from Mount Hope; yet none of them could distinguish who it was. Even if they had known the man, his face was simply too disfigured. Seeing nothing else around, no other evidence of what had happened, they reasoned together that the cause of death must have been an accident, a drowning. Then reasoning the proper thing to do, they dragged the body to the shore where they dug a shallow grave and buried it.

As they were finishing, one of the men stumbled upon a clutch of frozen ducks in the bent grass nearby; the birds were tied together with a leather strand, obviously the work of a hunter. A musket that lay near the birds, buried in the snow. No one recognized the weapon. But they determined to take it to Nemasket, the neighboring native village. Someone there might be able to identify the firearm and perhaps know of its owner.

* * *

Three natives entered Nemasket, the leader carrying the musket. A small crowd formed around them on the main road, inquiring as to their purpose in being there.

William Nahauton, then visiting among the elders, emerged from the main lodge, curious as to the activity, the presence of visitors. He stepped forward to greet the men, silently extending his hands. He took hold of the musket and turned it over, gently stroking the grain. He recognized it right away, the carved, mahogany stock and distinctive, silver lock plate. "Where did you get this?"

One man spoke, holding up the clutch of birds, "We found it with these beside Assawompset."

A second added, "We found the man. He was—he was under the ice."

William's face went white. He looked downward and wagged his chin. For more than a week he had been wondering what had become of his friend.

"We buried him beside the water's edge."

William let it sink in. He calmed himself. "Take me there."

They returned to Assawompset and easily found the grave, the mound of frozen earth amidst the trampled grasses. They exhumed the body to find it reasonably well preserved, but presently frozen stiff into the shape, the way that they had laid him in the hole. On seeing the clothing, William knew it was John Sassamon.

One of the men pointed out onto the pond, toward the spot where they had found him. "He must have fallen through, an accident."

"And his musket, and birds—you found them out there as well?" asked William.

"No. Here, in the grass."

William studied the men. He turned and took a closer look at Sassamon's swollen face, his frozen, gaping mouth. His eyes were locked in an upward gaze, showing only the whites.

A second added, "When we pulled him out, there was blood oozing from his neck. He must have cut it on the ice, as he fell through."

William said nothing. The facts were not adding up. His fears had come true. He stared at Sassamon and muttered, *"Now it comes."*

The three men looked at him, puzzled. But no one asked him what he'd meant.

3

William Nahauton had made up his mind. It did not matter what others thought. *Principle never yields to opinion. And the suggestion that what I am about to do violates who I am, goes against my nature—such is nonsense.* He had been mulling those thoughts for miles when he finally arrived in Marshfield, at the home of Governor Josiah Winslow. He concluded, *The outcome is out of my hands.*

William was greeted there at the door by one of the clerks, who escorted him inside and into the hall chamber. There sat the governor behind his desk, wearing his official white collar and black robe, presently engaged in his papers. A fire blazed beside him on the hearth, taking the chill off the afternoon.

On seeing his guest, Winslow set his pen down and rose to greet him, cordially tilting his head. "William. Nice of you to visit again." He pointed toward the open chair directly in front of his desk. "Make yourself comfortable."

William sat.

The governor grasped the edges of his robe and gracefully lowered himself into his chair, wearing his colonial nobility with such comfort. He swept his fingers down his flowing, brown locks and arranged them on his shoulders,

43

slender fingers that had not lifted a tool of labor since his privileged graduation from Harvard. *Funny,* William thought, *Sassamon also spent several semesters in Cambridge. The two men could not have been more different.*

The governor finished adjusting himself and leaned toward his guest, "You have something to report?"

William restrained his surprise, surprise at Winslow's choice of words, the implication that he had been on a mission, on some special assignment to the governor. He hadn't. He was there on his own accord, and he would not waste any time and get right to the point. "John Sassamon—" now reading the expectation on the Winslow's face, he continued his well-rehearsed opening line, "—Sir, his death—surely John was murdered."

Winslow studied William, from his native leggings to his feathered hair, pondering something. He spoke softly, "I am curious—why is it you came to *me?* Did you not think to go to Philip?"

William had expected this reaction; still it was hard for him to force his next line. "I, uh—I wish to see true justice."

"Justice, eh—" Winslow looked down at his papers, lifted one corner, momentarily distracted. He looked up. "I suppose you know Sassamon came to see me last month, just days before he disappeared."

"Yes."

"Hmm." Winslow cleared his throat. "He told me Philip was rallying his forces to attack the English settlements. And worse: that Philip was close to winning Narragansett support." He looked away. "I did not believe him. I can see now. I should have."

"And that is why I have come. I have found a witness, one not afraid of Philip. He saw it happen."

"Who?" The governor leaned forward. "Who is this witness?"

"Patuckson. He is Pokanoket."

"One witness in a capital crime?" He shook his head. "Is there other evidence? How did he die? Have you seen the body?"

"Yes. I have seen it. B-but it was frozen and disfigured. The wound you see, surely he bled to death, but it is not so clear as to the cause of the gash. Or perhaps he drowned. But surely there was a struggle, and a motive. John told me he feared for his life."

Winslow placed both hands firmly on his desk and pushed back. He rose and strolled several steps toward the fire, stroking his forehead. "I do not know why you have come to me. My father would never have adjudicated this matter. He would have said, 'This is Indian business,' and left it alone."

William rose to his feet. "John Sassamon was my friend. He was a preacher of the Word—the truth. If I do not pursue this matter, the truth will never come out." He stared at the governor till at last their eyes made contact. "And you *know* that to be so."

Winslow turned uncomfortably toward the flames. "Philip's father would have found you the truth."

The native wagged his head. He carefully selected his words. "I—I cannot seek Philip on this. He—he is surely *behind* the murder." He became insistent, "There is the body—the witness. You should seize this matter from me; pursue it legally. Then the truth will come out. Then there will be justice."

Winslow studied the fire, seemingly unmoved by the words, hypnotized by the orange flames. At last he took a breath and faced his native guest. Tightening his lips, he nodded his silent agreement.

Yet as the Englishman stared into the native's eyes, he could not help but fear where the politics would next take him. In his heart he knew, he knew this should have been an Indian matter. But then again, his was a new generation; New England was changing. The old ways of doing things, those were quickly fading.

4

Winslow had been anticipating this day for weeks. He was well prepared, having deposed his witnesses and interviewed the accused. His case was as solid as it could be. He had also thoughtfully planned the day, selected a venue and a jury, and put in place a process he was sure would help to smooth the way for the controversial verdict that was now so nearly in his grasp. He had advertised this event throughout New England, so that everyone would know the outcome, with nothing hidden. Even the weather was cooperating; it had turned out to be a spectacular day. He wondered to himself, *What could possibly go wrong?*

The governor and his seven assistants filed into their places in the court. They stood in two rows at the front of the modest sized, rectangular space. Beside them stood the jury, a panel of twelve Englishmen together with six Indians. Before them was the only piece of empty floor space, the well, which had a wooden podium raised at its center. Opposite the panel was the audience, a rabble of men, English and natives, together wedged into the tight space, even spilling out the door and onto the street. At the left was the table of the accused; behind it stood the three natives.

47

Sunlight flooded the room through the open windows at their back. The court reporter called for quiet and the room grew still in anticipation.

Judge Winslow read the indictment slowly, and with a loud voice, "We now have before us the trial of three Indians: Tobias, Wampapaquan, the son of Tobias, and Mattashunnamo. These three stand accused, that they did with joint consent this past January, at a place called Assawompset Pond, willfully, and of set purpose, and of malice of forethought, by force and arms, murder John Sassamon, another Indian, by laying violent hands on him and striking him, or twisting his neck until he was dead; and to hide and conceal this, their said murder, at the time and place aforesaid, did cast his body through a hole of the ice into said pond."

Then looking at the accused, the Judge asked them, "You have heard the charge. How do you men plead?"

The three stared at Winslow and the other judges standing beside him, keeping their silence.

"Gentlemen, do you plead guilty or innocent? Tell the court. How do you plead?"

Tobias looked at the other men, unsure of the process.

Winslow looked directly at him and spoke softly, "Tell the court, how do you plead: guilty or innocent?"

Tobias looked at Winslow, nodding his understanding, then looked again at his fellows before he spoke. "Innocent. I be innocent."

The two beside him nodded their heads. "Innocent."

A murmur swept the courtroom.

"We hear the plea," shouted Winslow to draw attention back to himself. "And now, Mister Prosecutor, you may address the jury." He waved toward His Majesty's Attorney, standing before the jury.

The prosecutor faced the jury, pointed at the accused, and spoke, "These three Indians: Tobias, Wampapaquan, and Mattashunnamo—these three Indians together stand accused of the murder of their fellow Indian, John Sassamon, this taking place this past January. You, gentlemen of the jury, both Englishman and Indian, you gentlemen—*you* will hear the evidence and decide the matter—that there might be justice." Then turning toward the three accused, he extended both hands toward them. "You defendants, you men may speak in your own defense."

Winslow nodded toward the prosecutor, then swept his eyes around the audience before he addressed the entire court, "You may all be seated."

All sat, except those men at the sides and back, against the walls where there were no benches. The room grew still.

Winslow continued. "Mister Prosecutor, call the first witness."

The prosecutor stood. "I call upon Jabez Howland."

A young Englishman pressed his way through the audience and entered the center of the well. He was smartly dressed, clean-shaven—a handsome man. He scanned around the room and made eye contact with his many acquaintances and friends. He climbed one step onto the podium, then was sworn in.

The prosecutor addressed Howland, "State for the court your occupation."

"I am constable for the Village of Middleborough."

"Now in that capacity, please tell us what you know of the remains of the victim, John Sassamon."

"Yes. As constable, I impaneled twelve men to exhume and did perform an inquest on the body—the body of John Sassamon."

"Do tell the court your findings."

"The body was in a rather sorry state, having spent many days under water, uh, beneath the ice of Assawompset Pond. It had been pulled from the frigid waters and buried in a shallow grave. By the time we did examine it—the body—it had been dead about four to five weeks. We had first to thaw the remains to give a proper examination, to commence to determine the cause of death.

"We noted the head in particular, the head was quite swollen; it being rather distorted in appearance. I believe this to be a coincidence of circumstance, the result of having been beneath the water for so long. There was no trauma, no evidence, nothing we could see on the head—that is, no marks or bruises such as would result from a violent blow. We saw no bruises on the body, the chest, back or legs. There were a few marks of putrefaction of the flesh, but these did not result from any wounds; as the body was merely in decay.

"Now the neck—the neck was another story. The neck had a large gash in it, making the head loose, loose as though the neck had been twisted—violently twisted I should say.

"Lastly, we sought to determine if the victim had drowned; or if he had been killed and then thrown beneath the ice. We found no water in the stomach or intestines. We saw no flow of blood or mucus from the nose. Finally, there were no excoriating marks on the fingers, marks such as would occur from scratching on the ice or the sand whilst trying to escape. And oh, yes—there was no frothy appearance around his mouth. None of these four evidences were present, which must make me conclude John Sassamon did *not* die by drowning."

The prosecutor kept the testimony moving. "And did you conduct any additional examinations on the victim?"

"Yes. We conducted a cruentation."

"A cruentation—Now please explain to the court the nature of this type of examination."

"Cruentation is a test to ascertain if the spirit of the dead might reveal the innocence or guilt of the accused."

"How is this test to be conducted?"

"The accused is brought near the body to see if there might be a reaction by the corpse, such as bleeding or other manifestation. When you conduct such a test there is not always a reaction, uh, which would only prove said test inconclusive. But if there *is* a reaction, these are duly noted and taken in as evidence."

"Tell us more. How did you conduct this test with the body of John Sassamon?"

"We could not bring all three of the accused to Middleborough, as two remained in jail here in Plymouth until now. But we did conduct the test with Tobias." Howland pointed at the defendant.

"The court notes that the witness has just pointed at the defendant." The attorney glanced at the court reporter, then continued, "So you brought Tobias near to the corpse? Do tell. Was there any reaction?"

Howland swallowed hard, then blurted, "The body started bleeding afresh from the neck, as if it had been slain again!"

A gasp swept the room. All eyes were on Tobias.

The accused sat straight-faced.

Winslow rapped his gavel, "Order! We must have quiet." He studied the three accused. Each sat stone-faced, silent. Winslow waited until the audience grew still. "Mister Prosecutor, please continue."

"This fresh bleeding—have you seen this before?"

"No."

"Is this the *'evidence'* you spoke of?"

"Please understand. I am not a doctor—*and I am not a minister.* I—I cannot say. I only know what I saw with my own eyes. I was following the process written in my mortuary guide book."

"You were following the procedures noted in the Mortuary Guide?"

"Yes."

"Alright then. Are you certain what you saw?"

Howland stiffened. "Of 'what I saw?' Yes. I am certain. But there is one more thing I must add, because you must know that I am not the superstitious sort. And I know that this is a matter of great import." He paused and looked out at the audience. "So on seeing the first result, I—I thought I must conduct a second test; just to be certain."

"A second test? Do tell. What was the result of the second test?"

Howland turned and stared directly at Tobias as he spoke. "I brought Tobias once more to the corpse. And just as before—the body did bleed afresh, as if newly slain."

The court responded aloud. Winslow pounded his gavel calling for quiet.

Tobias glared angrily at Howland.

The Englishman felt the heat of the stare; he brushed the hair from off his forehead and sat taller in his chair.

When the audience finally settled, the prosecutor continued. "Thank you, Mister Howland. That is all I have to ask. You are dismissed."

Howland got up, glanced at the defendants, then went back to his seat in the audience. His friends to either side smiled and tapped him on his shoulder. But he paid them no mind and sat very still, suddenly realizing the likelihood of a conviction pivoting on what he had just said, with all of Plymouth watching. He could feel his heart pounding. He didn't like how he felt.

The prosecutor turned toward the jury. "I would like to call the next witness." He scanned for the face among the crowd. "I call on the Indian, Patuckson."

The courtroom hushed as the native rose to his feet. He was a big man. He stepped sideways through the crowd and approached the podium.

The prosecutor held out a Bible.

"I am Christian. I will swear." He placed his hand on the book and made his oath to tell the truth.

"Mister Patuckson, err, Patuckson—Sir, do you know why you are here?"

"Yes. I here to tell what I see."

The prosecutor nodded. "And what did you see."

"I see John Sassamon kill'd."

"You did?"

Patuckson nodded. "I did."

"And where were you when you saw this killing?"

"I be followin' Tobias, Tobias an' others."

"Others? Do you mean the three men accused? Would you please point to whom you mean?"

Patuckson pointed to the three defendants.

"You were following the accused. Please continue."

"They set on killin' John Sausiman—so they followin' him. An' I follow' them—to see what happen."

"And what did you see?"

"Well it dark, an' cold—start to snow—an' I no see good. But then sky clear up an' moon come out. That when it happen."

"What happened?"

"Th-they attack him. One o' them grab Sausiman by neck and twist it—like this." He lifted his chin to the side and made a motion with his forearm across his chest.

"Then what happened?"

"I hidin' in woods, behin' tree n' scrub—an' while they grabbin' him—I—I move sum branches to look—that right when it snap—branch snap. I—I sure they hear—an' they gonna fine me an' throw me in ice too. I duck an' hide."

"Did you see anything else?"

"Yes. I fin'ly not afraid look—an'—an' I see them standin' at pond. They lookin' at ice—they done kill'd John and stuck him down that hole in ice. But I see where and what they done."

Tobias and Mattashunnamo shot to their feet and screamed, "Liar!"

"*Order! Order!*" shouted Winslow.

Tobias appealed, pointing at Patuckson. "This man lyin' thew his teeth. He no see *nuthin'*. He jus' wanna get even."

Winslow interrupted the prosecutor. He had not expected this change in the story, and was gravely concerned his case might fall apart. He looked at Tobias and intervened. "'Get even?' Please explain to the court."

"He be gamblin' with us an' he lose—so he made up this lie so he get even."

Patuckson looked at Winslow and then at the prosecutor. "No. No. No. You see this coat?" He grabbed his lapels. "These men give me this coat to shut me up from what I see. They lyin' now."

The prosecutor turned to Tobias. "What can you tell us about this coat?"

"That coat belong to Patuckson. He lose bet—he owe me silver. He give me coat instead. I tell him coat no good and give back. I wan' silver. He still gotta pay me silver."

The prosecutor glanced at Winslow, then looked at Tobias and Mattashunnamo. He needed to regain control of the testimony. "You men, be seated. I have more questions for this witness." He collected his thoughts and turned back to the witness, "Do you have any idea why these men would want to kill John Sassamon?"

Patuckson rolled his eyes. "Everyone know they be Philip's men—*Philip's close men*. They mad Sausiman tell Governor what Philip plan—that he hidin' guns, makin' ready to *war*."

The audience erupted. Several of the natives in the audience stood.

Winslow looked out into the crowd, seeing a mixture of surprise and anger in the many faces. This 'simple murder trial' was slipping out of his control, and he needed to get it back on script. He pounded his gavel, yelling, "We must have quiet, or I will have the room cleared!"

The room again grew quiet.

Winslow spoke, "Mister Prosecutor, please continue questioning the witness."

"So you say that the three accused were angry with John Sassamon, who told the governor of Philip's plans for war, and thus they wanted to silence him?"

"Yes."

"Can you tell the court? How would John Sassamon know Philip's secret plans for war? How would he know that?"

"Ole John—he be part Philip's men—on account he read an' write English tung. He live with Philip many years. He tell Philip English ways. Philip tell him many things too. John help Philip."

"So, John Sassamon knew Philip's secret counsels?"

"Yes." Patuckson nodded. "But not all."

"'Not all?' How is that?"

"Philip—he not trust John no more—on account o' words John write in Philip's will."

"Do you mean Philip's last will and testament?"

"Yes."

"Please explain."

"Philip ask John 'write his will' an' he tell John what to write. Well, John write Philip's words down an' some other words too, words leavin' lan' to John if Philip die. But John, he read back will to Philip an' not read that part. Later—later Philip—he fine out real words an' he real angry with Sausiman. So John run away."

"So Philip was angry that John had cheated him?"

Patuckson shook his head. "No. No. John no cheat. John marry Philip's niece—daughter of Tispaquin (husband of Philip's sister) —it only right she an' John get his lan'. They be related."

"I see. Tell me, is there anything else that might turn Philip against John Sassamon?"

"That ole John, he Prayin' Indian—like me. He try *years* convert Philip—make Philip Christian. That make Philip very angry—on account o' he hate Prayin' Indians. An' when he no trust John—he no need John no more read an' write. *Philip?* He wan' John Sausiman *dead*."

The courtroom groaned. All eyes turned toward the accused, three men silently sitting in the moment, blank-faced; men that now seemed swept along by a process they could not possibly comprehend.

The prosecutor faced the witness. "Thank you, Patuckson. I have no further questions. You may leave the court."

Patuckson stepped down from the podium and pushed his way up and out of the room. As he walked away, he kept his eyes focused on his feet, unable to look at any man. When he got to the doorway, he stepped outside and disappeared into the crowd.

The prosecutor glanced at Winslow and turned toward the defendants. "Do you gentlemen have anything to tell the court, to tell the jury?"

Tobias rose to his feet. "I no kill John Sausiman. That man, Patuckson, he liar. An'—an'—you can prove *no thing*. And John Sausiman? I don' know how he die. But these hands no kill John Sausiman. I be *innocent*."

The other two rose, "I innocent too."

"Me too."

All three nodded with conviction and sat back down.

Winslow rose to address the court, scanning the many faces in the audience, realizing the gravity of what had just happened, and his role in it. The rest would be a formality. He gave the audience the speech he had rehearsed, "We have heard the testimony of the witnesses, and we have heard the plea of the defendants. And now this is the proper matter, that we follow all law and ask this jury to decide whom to believe, and to reach a fair counsel based on the evidence that has been heard here today."

He turned toward the jury, needing now only to explain to the audience what he had devised. "You twelve Englishmen, you shall decide the fate of these defendants. Each of you will have a vote in the matter." He raised his voice as he looked toward the back row of the jury, so that even those standing outside the building could clearly hear him. "And you Indians: Hope, Maskippague, Wannoo, George, Wampye and Acoonootus—you men have been selected as the most indifferentist, gravest, and sage Indians—you shall be the witness of this proceeding to see that all this process is fair, seeking only the truth—so that all of Plymouth and its surrounding neighbors might have confidence in this court."

Winslow instructed the jury to enter the adjacent chamber where they might deliberate privately to decide the matter. They began to file out. He turned back to the audience and pounded his gavel. "This court is adjourned."

The governor watched the crowd as they turned toward the door and left. One man, William Nahauton, remained behind, standing.

The two men stared at each other silently as the room emptied. The trial *had* been so simple, so quick. Still, something about it had not felt quite right.

5

It had been cloudy all morning. The three convicted stood at the foot of the gallows, arrayed in a line, their hands bound behind their backs. A single rope draped from the wooden frame. Three ladders leaned against the crossbar.

The crowd had been gathering for hours. There were town folk and those who had traveled from miles away to witness the executions. There were men and women, Englishmen and native. Many of these had participated in an open-air worship service that morning and listened to the preaching of John Cotton, who had traveled down from Boston. This was an event not to be missed.

Governor Winslow stood on a makeshift platform: the bed of a cart. From there he addressed the crowd with a loud voice. "We are here today to carry out the sentence of the court. Last week we heard the trial and received the ruling of the jury, which I shall read for you:

'We, of the jury, one and all, both English and Indians, do jointly and with one consent agree upon a verdict: that Tobias, and his son Wampapaquan, and Mattashunnamo, the Indians, who are the

59

prisoners, are guilty of the blood of John Sassamon, and were the murderers of him, according to the bill of indictment.'

"And now it has been determined by the court according to the law that these men are to be hanged by the neck until their bodies are dead. And furthermore, the lands and personal property belonging to these convicted murderers, these are to be confiscated."

Facing the convicted he asked, "Do you gentlemen have anything to say?"

All three remained mute. Tobias glared at Winslow.

Winslow nodded to the hangmen, then climbed down from the wagon. He stepped over and into the crowd near to the gallows.

The two hangmen seized the arms of the first convict, Tobias, and led him to the center ladder. There, they helped him climb up two steps, to where they reached up and placed the rope around his neck. Then business-like, they climbed down and removed their ladders. Then they seized the legs of Tobias and flung them off his ladder, pulling it free and out of the way.

The crowd remained silent as Tobias swung and twisted beneath the murky sky, his shoulders and legs fell limp, fully yielded to his execution. Some of the spectators turned away. Others seemed transfixed by the slow spinning body. After a few minutes, the swinging stopped. The only action that remained was in the sentenced man's struggle to breathe as his face turned red and his eyes bulged from their sockets.

The twenty minutes it took Tobias to die seemed an eternity, with all of Plymouth watching in total silence— silence interrupted only briefly by the sound of men and women clearing their throats.

After Tobias was taken down, the next to be hanged was Mattashunnamo; and the process repeated itself. The big man died more quickly, only fifteen minutes. Still, it seemed far too long to many watchers. Those who had been standing at the fringes quietly turned and left, silencing their footsteps as much as possible. They had seen enough.

At last the execution time came to Wampapaquan. He was a young man, in his twenties, quite handsome, wearing feathers in his long black hair. He was led up the ladder, the rope was placed around his neck, and snugged. As before, the hangmen descended, removed their ladders, grabbed the legs, flung him off the rung, and quickly pulled the last ladder away. They had completed their duty, or so they thought.

Yet in that very moment, as the body swung free from the ladder, the afternoon clouds gave way and the gallows became bathed in sunlight. And as Wampapaquan dropped to the length of his noose, his rope snapped. The young man fell sideways to the ground, very much alive.

The crowd erupted, stirred awake from its stupor.

The hangmen hesitated, then ran to the convict. They seized him by the arms and helped him to his feet. Both turned and looked for Winslow, hoping for instruction. This failure of the rope had never before happened. Should they quickly get another rope?

Winslow stepped forward out of the crowd and approached the young native.

Wampapaquan's face was anguished with terror. His eyes darted at all the faces now surrounding and drawing closer. He fixed his eyes on the governor, opened his mouth, and blurted, "I tell you what they did, my father an' Mattashunnamo. I did no thing—but I see all they did. They kill'd John Sausiman. I tell you. *I tell you now!*"

Winslow turned around to the crowd, seeing it press in on them from all sides, in a ruckus, shouting aloud. He raised his hands to draw their attention, but to no avail. The scene was out of control. He turned back and studied the face of the Indian, the new confessor. *What to do?*

Winslow made his decision.

He motioned to the hangmen to shuttle the convict into the courthouse. He would move this discussion inside. There, he could hear the rest of the tale.

6

THE AFTERNOON OF JUNE 8, 1675

Two men walked the road that led away from Plymouth. For miles there was silence between the neighbors.

At last one of them spoke. "Well. Now we have justice. Uh, I mean, uh—now it is over. We can look forward to a new tomorrow. For that is all behind us."

The other stopped and stared at the ground. He thought a moment, hitched up his leggings, then reset his pace along the road, continuing in silence.

"Surely there was justice. For those men, those men had it coming to them. And then that rope—that rope had to break. I felt surely then that God had His hand in the matter. For did not that young man rise up and confess his innocence? Was it not a reprieve of righteousness? Had God not saved him?"

The other raised one eyebrow, he refocused on the path.

"But then the lies only continued—and it became obvious to the judge—even to the Indian jurors—and to all of us—that this young man was merely trying to save himself. For it was easy to confess that the other two—now dead—it was easy to lay all the blame on them. But instead, now we see the justice. For this young man is again sentenced to be executed; next week. I can understand they will take no more chance with that rope—he will be shot. Anyhow—that will lay the matter to rest. The matter will be over. Justice will be well served."

The second whispered, *"Justice."*

"Hmm. Yes. I am glad we can agree on that."

"Who said 'I agree?'" The second reached his hand up to his long, feathered hair; he flipped it behind his ear.

"So—so you don't agree?"

He put his open palm up. "I don't want to talk on it. I—I—" He let his hand fall. He sighed and reset his eyes on the path. He quickened his pace.

The first stopped. He thought a moment, then jogged to catch up, now matching his neighbor's stride.

"I can see how you might feel. For these, these were the first natives tried in our court. Why, why I suppose you would be right to feel that your people should handle these matters by your own means, as you always have. But these are not like our fathers' days. For now we are *one* land, with one system of God's justice. Do we not all do good to each other with one accord?"

The native's eyes flared. "We are *not* one. And your 'justice' is not ours. Those native jurors, they were not Pokanoket—they were *Praying Indians*. Besides, they had no say in the decision. It was—it was a play."

The English neighbor stopped. He stared unseeing at the path, then ran to catch up again.

"When the English first came, our king's father, Massasoit, he was as a great man and the English was as a little child. He constrained other Indians from wronging you English. He gave you corn and showed how to plant and was free to do good and let you have a hundred times more land—a *hundred* times more than now the king (Philip) has left for our people.

64

"But then it went wrong. For the English were the first to do wrong to our people.

"Our king's brother, Wamsutta, 'Alexander,' when he was king, he came miserably to die—being forced to Plymouth court and then was *poisoned.*"

"No. He was not *poisoned.* He—he was sick, and the governor tried to help. B-but he—he just died. You are just saying the lie that Philip says. For it is not true."

"*You English!* You do not know the truth. If twenty honest Indians testify an English did them wrong, it is nothing. But if one, *worst* Indian testify against any other Indian—or even Philip—when it pleases you English, *that* is enough!" He tossed his hands up. "When Philip sold you land, before you pay you would then say it was more than what was agreed, and a 'writing must be proof'—and some of you English, you made my people drunk—and when drunk, *then* you cheated them for no fair price!"

"Hold on. I do not understand. I have never heard of this before. W-why our fathers—your father, my father— they were good friends, and you and I have been good friends all our lives."

Both men stopped walking. They had reached a head in the trail, a place where the path divided.

The native took in a deep breath. "How many times have your horses and cattle come into our fields and *ruined* our corn—our food?"

"B-but you put no fences up to stop them."

"No fences?"

"You know the law. Your father knew the law. You must put up a fence to stop the animals. They are beasts. They cannot be controlled without a fence."

"The *law?* There is your *damn* law again. You English always go and hide behind your law—your law of *lies.* You keep guns for yourselves and take ours away. I cannot. I—I—"

The native put up his open palm. He stared at the ground and made a fist. After a moment, he relaxed his grip and let his hand fall to his side.

The two men turned and faced each other. In silence each studied the other's face.

The Englishman spoke, "Our fathers were good friends; and we have known each other all our lives. I have trusted you." He reached his hand across in a friendly gesture.

The native glanced at the empty palm, then turned away unflinching. Without a word, he set off down the trail to the right.

The Englishman watched his neighbor walk away. After a moment, he took the trail to the left.

Part One

7

Benjamin Church was shingling the roof of his new barn when he saw the two natives approaching through his field. From his vantage, he easily recognized one of them as Honest George. He watched them as they drew closer in the mid-morning sun, seeing them now waving frantically as they ran. He set his tools straight down and descended the ladder to greet them.

"Mister Church, Sir—" George spoke, out of breath. "—Awashonks like to meet you—right away."

He smiled and shook their hands, purposeful in his friendliness. "I shall be right with you."

Wasting no time to ask for explanation, Benjamin knew he would not have been summoned without good reason. He turned and ran into the main house, which was presently occupied by a tenant family, workers he had hired in the construction of his new plantation. There, he retrieved the eldest son, Charles Hazelton, to accompany him, since Charles well understood the native tongue. The four set off with haste toward the native village of Sakonnet, George at the front and Benjamin close behind.

While they were yet far away, the sound of drums filtered through the forest: a constant beat echoing through the air, a deep and dark sound, a rhythm that kept on building and gaining in strength. As they ran along, Benjamin kept his eyes fixed on the back of the native to his front, focused on his feet pounding upon the path, now in perfect rhythm with the drums. He felt a tightening of his stomach, haunted by the sound, because he already knew what was going on, a *protest over that ill-advised trial, those terrible executions in Plymouth.* And as the pounding of the drums continued to build, now joined by shouts, he knew this was the sound of resolve, the sound of preparation for war. His heart filled with dread.

On entering the native camp, he saw the festivities: hundreds of men and women had assembled, far more people than lived there normally, all dancing in a circle at the middle of the camp, their bodies painted as he had never seen, singing and moving to the beat of the drums. At the very center of the dance was Awashonks, the squaw sachem, wearing her royal dress; her arms and legs flailing energetically; her body glistening in the sun, all foamed in sweat.

Awashonks saw Benjamin arrive. She promptly broke off from the dance and stepped to the side, well away from the continuing frenzy. She drew her nobles around her and pointed at her visitor. She motioned that he should step forward and enter into her presence.

Benjamin approached with young Charles at his side. There they exchanged the customary compliments with all those present, then together, each took a seat. The shouting subsided and the drumbeat softened while the dance continued in the background.

Awashonks looked directly at Benjamin as she spoke in her native tongue.

The Englishman kept his eyes fixed on her as he listened to Charles' translations, first her words, then his response as they engaged together in conversation.

She began. "King Philip has sent six of his Mount Hope men here to draw us into a confederacy for war against the English. I would like your advice in the matter." The squaw leaned forward. "Philip says the 'Umpame' (the Plymouth men) have been gathering a great army to invade Philip's country."

Benjamin turned to Charles and stared into his young eyes for confidence in what he had just heard.

Charles nodded.

Benjamin gathered his thoughts. He examined the anxious faces of the warriors around him, seeing the magnitude of the moment. He focused on her face. "You know I will always tell you the truth—and you know how much I value our friendship—that I will give you always the best advice."

Awashonks, still sweating from the dance, took a long breath and calmed herself. "Yes. That is why I called you."

Benjamin softened his tone, knowing he was speaking for the benefit of all the witnesses. "I have just returned from Plymouth; just two days past. There, I met with the principal men of the government, for I am a member of the militia. I saw there no preparations for war. In fact, I had no discussions of war, and no thoughts of starting one." Benjamin perceived distrust on the faces of those listening. He would take a different tact. "You see that I have brought up goods for my home, that I am building a place to live, tilling the earth to plant. Now I ask you—would I do all this is if I was about to be at war with you, my close neighbor?"

Awashonks leaned toward him, nodding pleasure at his words. She scanned the faces of her nobles, intending to leverage his words to still their resistance. "I believe you, Mister Church. You are a trustworthy man."

She leaned to the side and whispered to one of her men, who promptly rose and left. She turned back to Benjamin, "I would like you to speak with the Mount Hope men. They are still here."

In a few moments, six natives filed into where they were seated. Their hair was waxed straight up in combs, their faces painted, and their bronze muscles glistening with sweat. As they entered, their eyes glared in a singular direction, aimed at Benjamin, the Englishman, the stranger in their midst. Their mouths stayed shut, yet there was no mistaking their hatred. They did not sit.

Benjamin rose and stepped close to them. Each man wore on his back a powder horn, and a leather pouch full of shot. They stood tall and straight, flexing their muscles, eyes fixed on Benjamin as he pressed between them. They measured each other.

Awashonks broke the silence. "These Mount Hopes, they say that unless I enter into Philip's confederacy for war, that they will privately kill your English cattle and burn your houses on this side of the river; so that you and your Englishmen might come and fall on me and my people, thinking we are the authors of the mischief."

The Mount Hopes snapped their glare at the squaw sachem.

Benjamin reached up and seized one warrior's shot bag, then stared into his face. "What are these bullets for?"

The native sneered in English, "To shoot pigeons."

His comrades laughed.

Benjamin turned to Awashonks and spoke firmly, "If Philip wants war, your best hope is to knock these Mount Hopes on the head, and to shelter yourself with the English."

Two of the Sakonnets lurched at Benjamin. One named Little Eyes taunted, "I would speak to you in private—here—in the bushes." He tilted his head toward the woods as his lips curled into a drooling grin.

Honest George and several friends stood and pressed themselves between the men, sheltering Benjamin.

Several of the natives raised their voices with angry words. They drew close to George and Benjamin. Others jumped to their feet, now snarling. Those protecting Benjamin howled back and everyone began to form sides. The sides exploded.

Undaunted by the scene, Benjamin leaned forward in the arms of his protectors. He yelled at the Mount Hopes, "You bloody wretches! You thirst for the blood of your English neighbors—men who have *never* injured you—but who have abounded in kindness to you. I tell you—though I desire nothing more than peace—if nothing but war be your aim, then I shall be to you a sharp thorn!"

The crowd grew quickly out of hand. More of the friendly natives closed in tight, surrounding Benjamin and his young translator, for they feared for their safety. At the same time, those in favor of war grew louder as their numbers swelled, joined by those who had left the dance. They pushed toward Benjamin, threatening to tear him in two.

Awashonks leapt to her feet and pressed herself into the middle of the throng, forcing her way toward her guest. She drew up close and confided through Charles. "Mister Church, I like your advice."

Benjamin realized then the panic of the moment, for the mob had surged beyond even the squaw sachem's ability to control it. He fixed his eyes squarely on hers.

She spoke to him in English. "You must go Plymouth, warn your government."

Benjamin pleaded. "But you must not join in this rebellion. This will surely prove fatal to you and to your people."

The ground was now shaking and their voices could no longer be heard. Benjamin and Awashonks stared at each other. They shook hands.

"Go now!" She shouted and shoved Benjamin on his way. She grabbed several of her most trusted men and pushed them along with him, telling them to guide him safely back to his home.

Pressed along by Awashonks' men, hustled out of the camp, Benjamin turned and looked back over his shoulder. He saw the dance resume. It was even louder than before.

8

Benjamin made ready to depart his farm, ignoring the pleas of his native protectors, pleas that he should first secret his possessions away, to protect them from the looming vandals. But he wanted to do nothing of the sort—that was his means to express his will, to show confidence that war could be avoided. Nevertheless, to prove his trust in their friendship, he directed the men to a spot in the woods where they might later hide his possessions, should they see any vandals approach.

Feeling now the urgency to depart, to deliver the message to the governor, Benjamin saddled his horse and mounted. He pleaded to the Sakonnets as they stood by him. "Tell Awashonks to maintain her trust in the English." Then not at all sure he would be able to do so, he spoke out of hope. "I will return to her soon."

Benjamin set off for Plymouth, burdened with worry.

Ten miles to the north, he entered the territory of the Pocasset, which ran along the eastern bank of the Sakonnet River, beside the narrows with Aquidneck Island. He dismounted at a small stream of fresh water that trickled down into the bay, there to water his horse.

As his horse rested, Benjamin drank in the scenery. To the north, the narrows opened up to the wide Mount Hope Bay. Opposite him, a skinny peninsula of Aquidneck Island (Rhode Island) extended far out into the bay, above which he could see across the expanse to Mount Hope on the horizon, the place of the Pokanoket, Philip's home.

As he stood there, refreshed by the beauty of the sun sparkling on the vast blue bay, he noticed the shadow of a lone figure in a canoe far out on the water. He stayed fixated on the figure, paddling sure and hard, speeding his canoe around the peninsula and then turning south, directly toward him. As it drew closer he recognized the native in the stern of the little boat. It was Petonanuet, the current husband of the queen of Pocasset (her first husband had been Wamsutta, Philip's brother). Benjamin waved and Petonanuet happily returned the signal.

Petonanuet came ashore and pulled his canoe high onto the strand. He came up happy to greet Benjamin, who was standing at the top, waiting for him. But the native's smile quickly faded when he saw the expression on the Englishman's face. He held out his hand and took a firm hold of Benjamin's. "What is wrong, my friend?"

"I just came from Awashonks. Philip's men were in the camp, inciting for war."

Petonanuet placed his hand on Benjamin's shoulder and sighed. "Not surprised. I jus' came from Mount Hope. They been dancin' for weeks." The last of his smile vanished. "War is certain."

Benjamin's body shivered at the words.

"Natives were there from all parts—and Philip—Philip expected to go to Umpame (Plymouth) to testify 'bout Sausiman."

Benjamin could not believe what he was hearing. "How do you know this?"

"Two men come to Mount Hope while I was there: James Brown of Swansea and Samuel Gordon. They bring a letter from Governor Winslow. And two other men come from the Massachusetts Bay with another letter. They want to hear from Philip.

"Now the young Mount Hopes got angry, they wanna' kill James Brown and the others. But Philip, he not allow it, on account his father charge him to 'show kindness to Mister Brown.' Then after the men leave, and because there was so much anger over the letters, Philip had to promise these young Mount Hopes, promise they could rifle empty houses of the English and kill cattle—on Sunday, when the English go to meeting."

"This Sunday?"

"Yes."

Petonanuet stared at Benjamin, seeing the impact of his words on his friend. "Will you come up, see my wife?"

Benjamin nodded.

The two men turned and walked up the hill and into the village of the Pocasset. They approached the queen's lodge, which was at the center of the camp, a camp that was hauntingly quiet, as there were few natives in sight. Weetamoo, the queen, stood outside her home, alone, watching them approach.

Benjamin extended his hand to her in a familiar greeting.

Weetamoo looked into his blue eyes. She smiled at him and shook his hand, then lifted her gaze all around the camp. Her eyes filled with sadness. "They all gone. They with Philip—*dancin'.*" She caught her breath. "Now there be war—*damn* war."

Benjamin, yet dazed with denial, surged suddenly awake, recalling his hope. "But you do not have to join him. You can go across to the island; secure yourself there and your people. Governor Winslow, he is your friend. He will not harm you."

The queen leaned toward Benjamin. She admired his handsome face, studying the cleft in his clean-shaven chin. Her eyes drifted down to his fine white linen shirt with its wrought silver buttons, a testament to his English wealth. She turned away.

"Please. You must cross over to the island. I will go to the governor, to tell him of your loyalty. He will protect you from Philip's madness."

She stood, looking away, vainly concealing her gloom.

Benjamin realized there was nothing more he could say, and time was wasting.

He bid them both a hasty goodbye, climbed back up onto his horse, and left the village, following the trail as it turned to the northeast, toward Plymouth.

Now driven by the urgency of forces fast erupting beyond his control, Benjamin rode hard the rest of the way there. He had to warn his people. And as he leaned forward in his saddle, Weetamoo's distancing doubt stayed ever at the forefront of his mind.

9

A band of Pokanoket natives marched north from Mount Hope, out onto the neck where it joined to the mainland. From there they turned east, keeping off the path, careful to conceal themselves amidst the trees. Soon they came upon the English settlement at Swansea. It was early yet, so they waited, waited for the settlers to depart their houses to attend church, knowing well the colonials' custom for Sundays, "the Lord's Day."

Their action would be swift; in and out before there could be bloodshed. For they believed in their hearts, and by superstition, that the side that was first to kill would surely be conquered. With this belief set firmly in their minds, they entered unmolested into vacant houses, stole goods, set fire to barns, and shot several cows, all without seeing a single settler. Having done their damage, they vanished into the woods, disappearing before the colonists could see the smoke rise, but having at last put action to their many years of frustrated words. These young ones, these ambitious, intended that others of their kin would surely join them now; emboldened by this undertaking. These actions would awaken their allies and certainly enlarge their force. That was the plan.

When several of the natives returned again to Swansea two days later, they found farms abandoned, as the settlers had fled to safety in the village garrisons—log homes that had been "hardened" with heavy wooden shutters protecting the windows and doors. Each such fortress was large enough to house several frightened families.

Now confident to roam the abandoned properties uncontested, the natives pillaged all the more.

Yet not all farms were left unwatched.

Fearful of the loss of his possessions, an elderly settler returned to inspect his property, accompanied by his grandson. Crossing his field toward the house, he spied the front door ajar. He shouted and ran toward the house, hustling to secure his goods.

The old man's screams alerted the invaders, who were yet inside. Two natives rushed out of the door, turned and fled. A third, a young man, tumbled out of a window and fell to the ground.

The old man yelled to his grandson, "Shoot!"

The young native scrambled to his feet, but fell at the sudden report. He had been shot. But the wound did not prevent him from escaping.

Later that day, three Pokanokets approached the garrison owned by Reverend John Myles. From a safe distance, they yelled unrelenting at the boarded windows. "Why did you shoot? Why did you shoot at us?!"

The reverend opened the door and stepped outside, unafraid to greet them. He took several steps forward onto the lawn and studied their faces, to see if he knew any of them.

The young man that had fired the first shot came and stood at the reverend's side, carrying his musket. He planted both feet firmly on the ground and raised the stock to his shoulder, pointing it directly at the Indians.

The reverend placed his hand firmly on the barrel and shoved it toward the ground. He scowled at the youth, then looked across at the natives. "Is your young man alive?"

The Indians seethed. *"He's dead!"*

The lad stared at the ground and uttered, "It is no matter."

But to the natives it *was* a matter. It was a great matter.

10

The governor and leaders of the churches had declared that Thursday the 24th was to be a day of public humiliation throughout the colony of Plymouth, a time for prayers and fasting, appealing to God for protection for his people.

Four days later, Captain Church and his company were at the forefront of those that marched into Swansea in the afternoon; sent ahead as scouts to a larger force commanded by Captain James Cudworth of Scituate, under the supreme command of Major William Bradford, Jr. Their purpose at Swansea was to be a police presence, to secure the village, to protect the residents against harm and loss of property.

Everything seemed to be happening too fast, and now out of Benjamin's control. His words with the governor had only added another log to the flames already burning when he had arrived in Plymouth, where many other voices had assembled and were scrambling to fight a war that had not yet even started. He had just returned to his plantation, right when the express arrived, telling him to muster his neighbors, family members, and a few friendly Indians to Taunton, to join there with some two hundred others who had been called to arms, to defend the colony. What else could Benjamin do but leave immediately, and assume his responsibility as a sworn member of the militia? At least then he could see the action with his own eyes and be in some position to shape what was going on; there to work in some way, any way to keep his promises to his native friends. He'd had no time to stop and see Awashonks before he departed for Taunton, and that bothered him greatly.

It took so long to assemble, and then two more days to march to Swansea, that Benjamin feared they were already too late to prevent the coming wave of violence. The full eclipse of the moon they witnessed during their march, the sight of seeing the disk turn the color of blood, gave the entire troop a sense of ominous foreboding. And the sudden foulness of the weather that came with the morning, the gathering swirling winds, caused the superstitious among them to fear that God was against their enterprise.

They came at last upon Swansea, a village that was bathed in silence. They marched passed burned-out houses and dead cattle lying in the grass. Not a person was in sight. Benjamin and his men feared the worst.

At last they found the villagers had sequestered themselves in two garrison houses not far from each other, one belonging to Major Brown, the other to John Myles.

The moment the militia arrived, the residents streamed outside to greet them, all in a panic. The men wore grave expressions and the women and children were crying. They pressed in against Benjamin and his men, seizing hold of them, grabbing at them in speechless embrace, like they were greeting long-lost relatives.

Before Benjamin had a chance to inquire as to the source or reason of their trouble, words flew desperately from their lips. More of them poured out of the garrison door and began to shout over each other. They wailed of attacks, pillaging, people fired upon, and most troubling, some of their men were missing.

Minutes later, the other militia companies flooded in to join them. The scene turned into a mob, with no sense of who was in charge or exactly what had happened. And before any sense of order could be restored, before even they could assemble to hear the facts, the sound of guns rang out.

Two of the English sentinels fell down dead.

Chaos ensued.

Bullets flew, people ducked and stumbled, some tried to run, some reached for their weapons, and fumbled to load them. *But where to aim?*

Smoke rising from the tree line revealed the assassins. No time to reload, a group of natives was seen taking flight into the woods.

Captain Thomas Prentice, who was standing behind Benjamin at that moment, grabbed Benjamin's shoulder and shouted, "Get your men and come with me!" He gestured toward two of his quartermasters who were standing by the horses, and barked at Benjamin, "Go with those two!"

Benjamin quickly rounded up his men. But by the time they had mounted, quartermasters Gill and Belcher and a group of others were already well out ahead of them, in hot pursuit of the criminals.

Setting off to the west, Benjamin and his men crested a short rise and descended the trail toward the river, their horses huffing along at full speed, kicking up clods.

Approaching Myles' bridge, Benjamin heard the barrage of muskets. Now with the scene in view he could see the outlaws to the left, on the far side of the river, hiding in the trees. To the right he saw the militia's horses behind a group of trees. He dismounted quickly and ran ahead to join his army, where they lay hiding in the weeds. The gunfire continued.

He looked out at the center of the scene. There were several men from the forefront of the first wave, victims of the ambush. Thomas Hammond sat motionless on his horse, slumped over in his saddle. His animal stood in the center of the bridge, blocking traffic. Behind Hammond, Belcher lay on the ground, his horse having been shot out from under him. Third in line was Mister Gill.

As he watched, Gill was struck in the rubs with a ball. The fabric of his coat exploded in a cloud. Gill grabbed his side and heaved forward in the saddle, yet he continued. He reached down, grabbed Belcher, and threw him across his saddle, then spun around and rode back up to join them. There, the men gingerly helped both men down and examined them.

Belcher had taken a ball in his leg. Gill was still holding his arm tight to his side, grimacing in pain. He lifted the arm, which revealed a gaping hole in his buff coat. Through the hole was a great wad of paper. He pulled it away slowly, fearing the worst; amazed, there was no blood; the skin had not been broken. He pressed his hand in and stroked his tender ribs.

The natives had re-loaded and the gunfire resumed. Bullets whizzed through the trees about their heads as the sky grew dark and the winds began to swirl; a thunderstorm was upon them and many of the men shouted profane oaths to God. One of the men, a stout man who'd marched in with a troop from Watertown, overwhelmed by the moment, simply broke. He jumped on his horse and fled the scene. Several of the others turned toward their animals, eager to escape with him, willing to leave poor Hammond behind, for they presumed he was dead.

But Benjamin would have none of it. He rose and stomped after them, yelling, "How can you go and leave the wounded!"

Benjamin ran to his horse and flung himself up into the saddle. He spun his animal in the direction of the bridge and made ready to ride out from cover.

But before he had a chance to leave, Gill cried out, "Wait for me!" forgetting his ribs. A third joined with them and the three rode in a hurry out from the trees and down onto the causeway.

By the time they got onto the bridge, Hammond had fallen to the ground, dead.

Benjamin dropped from his mount and picked up the body. He laid it across the front of Gill's saddle, then turned for Hammond's horse, which had wandered off the far end of the bridge; the animal was headed out onto the neck, directly toward the outlaws. In no mood to let the horse get away, Benjamin handed the men his bridle and took off running.

As Benjamin crossed the bridge he could clearly see the natives. They had fallen back, but now were returning to his right, back to their positions. He counted eight.

Benjamin ran, seized hold of the horse, and spun back toward his men. He waved his arms and pleaded to everyone. "Come on!"

While he was calling, the whole of the outlaws discharged their weapons at him in one loud clap.

Every shot missed.

Benjamin ran now unmolested back to join his men, pulling the horse, finding all of his men cowering in the trees. He studied their faces. He knew that none of them had ever fired a gun at another man. He counted them; two-dozen farmers and fishermen. He turned toward the band of vandals, then faced his brothers and seethed. "*Lord have mercy on us* if such a handful of natives should dare such an army as ours."

Benjamin's men straightened. They loaded their guns and took aim toward the outlaws. Their muskets exploded.

The natives took flight. One was seen limping, having been struck in the foot.

Fear faded from Benjamin's men. They rose up and rode together out from the trees, down and over the bridge. There they divided their force: one group set off to the right, another to the left, a third held the center.

Not long into the forest, the band on the right wing fell under fire. One of their young men was hit, Ensign Savage. As soon as he took to yelling, the gunfire suddenly stopped, for it was fast understood he had been shot by one of his own men, from the group in the center. Dreading further disorder, the three groups rejoined as one, relieved to learn that the young man had only a flesh wound.

Farther south, they came to a narrow part of the neck, a place the natives called Keekamuit. The area was sparse of vegetation, with clear views ahead and over to the water to the east a safe distance. The native canoes that had often filled this shore were long gone. Philip and his army had abandoned Mount Hope.

But the Indians had not left without leaving a message there for them, a message that Benjamin and everyone with him that saw it could not possibly mistake. A grove of eight poles had been pounded into the sand. Skewered atop each was the head of an English victim. Their remaining body parts lay mutilated on the ground all around, left in grizzly crimson circle. The missing Englishmen of Swansea had been found.

Benjamin knew then that Philip's men were no longer merely criminals. They were no longer just the vandals of Swansea. Now they had gone too far.

11

The other members of the militia arrived and crowded around the massacred remains. Each man was anxious to get a look and each recoiled at the ghastly sight and putrid stench; the body parts were swarmed with flies. They spun around and looked back up the trail, then all around them, fearful of the next attack. They gripped their guns with dread.

Calmer heads needed to prevail. Benjamin ordered several of the men to take down the pikes and to gather the body parts together for a proper burial. In the meantime, several of the other officers came into the scene. Benjamin overheard them assess the situation, stating the obvious, that Philip's men had staved their drums and quit the neck, having conveyed their canoes to the east side of the bay.

Benjamin approached Prentice, as several of his captains and junior officers did the same. They quickly engaged in planning their next move. He stood to the back and listened.

"We need to hold fast this ground, ground we have gained."

"Yes. We should build a fort."

89

The fort idea quickly took hold. They all nodded their heads.

By now, several scouts had returned from examining the empty wigwams in Philip's camp, which eased their immediate concerns. The enemy was completely gone.

Benjamin forced himself into the conversation. "Philip's men have gone over to the Pocasset side to engage those Indians with him in this rebellion. We must pursue them, before they gather reinforcements."

They shook their heads.

"But we have gained this ground."

"And have beaten them out of here."

"Now we have need to hold it."

The desperation in their faces revealed their true motive: fear, fear of engagement.

Benjamin was shocked by their poor judgment. He had been at the forefront of the first action; there had barely been a fight. If the natives had fled Mount Hope, it was not on account of being forced away. There was no ground that had been "gained." It was obvious to him that the natives had left by choice, for the Swansea men had been dead for more than a day. This was a planned display of what was to come. He studied his fellow militia leaders, men ill equipped for war; men naïve to the gravity of their station—to protect their fellow countrymen. Yet realizing their fears in the moment, he sensed he must disagree with care, not to put them off, to attack their weakness, or to offend them with brash words. He gently repeated himself. "But they have only left here to strengthen themselves. We must follow after them now, before they are able to accomplish their goal."

Benjamin's words had no chance; they were drowned out in disagreement that grew harder by the second. But he'd had his say. Now he would shrink back and keep his thoughts to himself. He did not want to make enemies.

The leaders assembled and formed a grand council. They fast resolved that two-dozen men should stay there and hold the ground. Orders were then given for the rest to march to Rehoboth to regroup there with the other militias.

The whole of the ten mile march north, Benjamin played out in his mind what he might say to influence his leaders to change their direction, for he could not help but feel that opportunity for a fast ending to the conflict was slipping between their fingers. At the same time, he fretted about his promise to Awashonks, seeing he was already delayed in getting word to her. *Will she side with Philip and join in the madness?*

At Rehoboth, the Plymouth and Rhode Island militias met up with an army that had marched down from Boston under the leadership of Captain Samuel Mosley. All the captains gathered at the meetinghouse, in the presence of Majors Cudworth and Bradford.

After several had described to the high command what had taken place at Swansea, they made their pleas to return to Mount Hope to construct the fort, and to man it against the potential return of Philip to his home. The matter was quickly agreed and settled. The order of business then moved on to matters of command and supplies for the army.

The commissary general for the Army, Constant Southworth, Benjamin's father-in-law, promptly retired his post. At the age of sixty, he was no longer fit for exertion in the field, and even wearier of the impossible task of raising provisions for the militia. He put forward Benjamin to be his replacement.

Benjamin stepped forward to accept the position. And seizing the momentary power of his troubling new post, he unleashed his objection to the plans that had just been approved; for to him they were plans to build a fort *for nothing.* "Gentlemen. I was at the forefront of the conflict.

The enemy was not beaten out of Mount Hope neck—though it was true that they fled. Yet they fled before we even pursued them. They did not leave by our sword or guns; they left rather to strengthen themselves, and to gain a more advantageous post." Benjamin studied the worried opposition in all their eyes. He pressed deeper. "I urge you, we must move over to the Pocasset side, pursue the enemy, and kill Philip." He let his words sink in. "This would, in my opinion, be more probable to keep possession of the neck, than to waste our army there to build a *fort*. I tell you, some of the Indians, and not a few, have pleased themselves with the fancy of a mighty conquest that will bring down all of us."

Bradford pushed himself back onto the floor, taking back control of the meeting. He focused on Benjamin, a man who had married into his family, since he (Bradford, Jr.) and Constant Southworth were half-brothers by the same mother, Alice Carpenter. He placed his hand on Benjamin's shoulder as he looked out at the other captains, a dozen men, knowing full well that every one of them was a volunteer and unaccustomed to war. He made ready to gently dismiss Benjamin's brave plan.

Yet before Bradford could open his mouth, Captain Matthew Fuller raised his voice. Fuller was an older man, a respected physician. "I agree with Mister Church. Philip is the source of this trouble. We must cut out this cancer, before it spreads to the whole body."

Several were heard to grumble.

Benjamin added, "And we must consult with the Sakonnet and Pocasset Indians, for neither of their queens want war. They share no love for Philip."

Bradford studied Fuller's face, mindful of the man's twenty years of service in the militia. In his post as surgeon to the Plymouth Army, he was a man of experience and wisdom. He thought a moment, then made a decision. "Very well then. Matthew, you shall lead a group of six files across the bay in pursuit of Philip. And you shall take Mister Church with you as your second, to seek any conversation you can have with the Pocasset or Sakonnet Indians. The rest of you shall go under the command of Major Cudworth and build the fort." He gave the rest of the details of his orders to everyone and the meeting concluded.

As the men filed out, Fuller approached Benjamin. "Are you truly willing to engage in this enterprise?"

Benjamin nodded wholeheartedly. "Indeed. But I do think we should have had more men assigned."

Fuller leaned forward and spoke softly, "You know, I am ancient and too fat for this. I fear the travel and exertion will be too much for me." He was seventy.

Benjamin, a hardy man of thirty-five years, placed his hand on Fuller's shoulder. "It will not be so hard. I will be helping." He smiled. "And God will be watching over us." Benjamin would gladly have led the men alone and excused the old man of his hardship and travels. But the orders had not permitted such. He needed Fuller. He would rather do anything in the world than to stay and build a fort.

12

Fuller and Benjamin had drawn out the number assigned to them, thirty-four men. They marched the same night to the ferry, which transported them under the cloak of darkness to the north end of Aquidneck Island (Rhode Island). From there, the next night, they took passage over to the Pocasset side in Rhode Island boats, landing at Howland's Ferry. There, they divided their force in two and set off before sunrise on foot, hoping to surprise some of the enemy by falling onto one of their camps.

Later in the morning, under the heat of the sun, the two groups turned and reunited at the appointed spot. There, Benjamin explained that his men had not found any tracks. He asked Fuller for his report.

Fuller looked down. He hesitated. "Well, um. After we had walked a ways, and while it was still dark, several of the men started a small fire so that they could have a smoke." Fuller watched Benjamin's face curl up as he delivered the news. "Some of the enemy saw us—uh—we saw them run away. We ruined the element of surprise."

Benjamin composed himself. He could hardly yell at a superior officer. He put his hand on Fuller's shoulder, not wanting to make him feel bad. "That's alright."

Feeling a change in subject was best, Benjamin looked for the man he had put in charge of breakfast. He saw where he was seated and walked over to him. "We are going to have our breakfast now."

The soldier stood up and held his hands out. "Captain, sir—uh—I don't have it."

Benjamin blinked. "You don't have it?"

"I am sorry, sir. It was late. Sir, we had been up all day, and, well—well, I fell asleep. A-and, then when the boat was about to leave, well, one of the men shook me awake, and I got straight up and ran right onto the boat. A-and, I left the food there."

Benjamin stared at him.

"Sir. I forgot to bring it with me."

Benjamin pursed his lips and shook his head. He thought a moment, then looked at the soldier. "That's alright." He squeezed his shoulder and smiled. "I have something."

Benjamin retrieved his pack. The day before, Madam Cranston, wife of the former deputy governor of Rhode Island, had generously given him two cakes of rusk (twice-baked bread). He pulled these out and divided them among the men. That was all the provision they had.

After their slender breakfast, Benjamin talked with Fuller of resuming their search for Philip's men, for he was anxious to fulfill their purpose. One of the bright young soldiers overheard the conversation and approached him. "With all of the talk on the other side of the river, Mister Church, you have yet to show us any Indians."

Several of his friends drew close around him, listening.

Benjamin studied them. They were young, full of ambition, yet fearlessly naïve. They could not possibly recognize the hazard that lay before them, a hazard magnified by having so few of them to face an enemy emboldened by the ease at which they had acquired fresh blood on their hands. He looked at them straight-faced. "If you desire to see Indians, I am sure you shall soon be seeing Indians enough."

Benjamin and Fuller again divided the force. Benjamin drew off fourteen men, leaving the majority to go with Fuller, to help protect the old man.

Benjamin's group set off south along the east bank of the river, heading toward the village of the Sakonnet. They eventually discovered a fresh and plain track at the place where a stream ran into the Nannaquaket neck; they followed it to the east, away from the main waterway, seeing that it was leading them toward the great pine swamp.

Benjamin turned to his men. "If we follow this track, no doubt we shall soon see Indians enough." They expressed their willingness to enter the swamp.

Not far into the woods, one of the men narrowly escaped the bite of a rattlesnake. Moments later, a second screamed at the sight of another rattler, coiled and ready to strike. Now with all eyes focused downward at the path, scouring between the grass and weeds, they spotted more of the brown, patterned reptiles slithering among the dead leaves. They had stumbled into a nest of snakes.

With urgency of purpose, they backed out of the woods, more fearful of the reptiles that haunted that place than the Indians they had been pursuing.

They reset their course southward, past Nannaquaket pond, then veered back toward the bank of the Sakonnet River, keeping the water always on their right. After an hour, they came down onto the Punkatees neck. There they found a large abandoned wigwam, full of Indian possessions and supplies. Several of the young men began to load up their arms, happy to seize the plunder. But Benjamin forbid it. "Your hands will soon be full with other business."

They crossed the head of a creek that emptied into the river there and again discovered fresh Indian tracks. They followed these along the top of the riverbank to a piece of property that Benjamin was familiar with, property owned by his neighbor, John Almy, the same man who had sold him his own land, which lay just to the south of where they stood. Ahead was the fence that surrounded Almy's peas field. They kept low following the tracks, scurrying undiscovered up to the fence.

Benjamin divided his group into two parties. He sent one group with David Lake around the field to the left, since Lake was acquainted with the land on the other side. He led his group to the right, around the perimeter of the field.

Two Indians were seen coming across the peas field toward Benjamin's men.

Benjamin and his group fell flat to the ground, undiscovered.

But Lake and his men did not use the same caution.

The Indians saw them, turned, and ran.

Benjamin jumped up and called to the natives. "Hullo there! I'd like to speak with you. We will not hurt you." He tumbled over the fence, scrambled up, and ran after them.

But the natives bolted to the fence on the far side of the peas field and leaped over it. One of them turned and fired his piece toward Benjamin. It missed. Benjamin spun around and looked back at his men. No one had been hit.

One of Benjamin's men blew past him and ran right up to the fence. He stopped, took aim, and fired his musket.

One of the two Indians was heard yelling.

Benjamin ran the rest of the way across the field and stood beside his man. He found himself conflicted, wanting to chastise his man for shooting, but at the same time he recognized he and his men had been fired upon first—his soldier's reaction had been a natural act of self defense. They both studied the slope above them. Neither Indian was in sight; they had vanished into the thickets that covered the side of the hill.

"I think I got him," said the young man, proudly.

Benjamin summoned the rest of the men. They climbed together over the fence and continued their pursuit, heading through an open area, up toward the woods. Because they were out in the open, he spread his men out to make them appear as a large show of force. Benjamin took the lead.

But before they had a chance to see anyone, they were saluted with a volley from fifty or sixty guns. Some of the bullets came very close to Benjamin.

He turned to look, expecting to see half his men lying dead. But he saw them all still on their feet. *"Thank God!"* he uttered. They quickly took aim and began firing their weapons toward the trees, in the direction of the smoke.

Gathering his thoughts, Benjamin yelled at his men, "Don't all fire at once!" For he knew that if they had, the natives would run unopposed at them with their hatchets.

Benjamin directed them to retreat to the fence, over it, and back into the peas field. He put half his men under the fence with their muskets loaded, and sent the rest farther out into the middle of the field where they could stand to recharge their guns. He hoped to draw the natives toward the men standing in the open, only to be surprised by those left hiding under the fence.

But turning his eyes to the ground that lay above them, the hillside seemed to move. It was covered with Indians, with the barrels of their guns glinting in the sun. They were running in a circumference, intending to surround them.

Seeing they were about to be overcome, Benjamin remembered the boats that had been ordered to come and fetch them away, wondering where they were. He looked over his shoulder, beyond the field and down to the river, then across to the other side, about a mile distant. He could see the boats there at Sandy Point, along with a number of horses and men. He focused his eyes at the near bank and wondered how he could get his men down there to be rescued. He spied a section of a stone wall near the water, pointed, and yelled at Lake, "Go for that wall, and take as many with you as you can!" They had to move, and now.

He turned to the men around him and took off his jacket. "Quick! Strip to your shirts." Then he ordered for three distinct shots to be fired, for he hoped their friends on the other side of the river might notice them as Englishmen.

One at a time they worked their way through the peas and down the hill, white shirts gleaming in the sun, all the while taking turns to fire back up the hill into the enemy, slowing their attack.

Now at the bottom, Benjamin waited for the last four men to come and join them. About twenty yards from the wall they stopped to eat some of the peas, being very hungry. The enemy rained on them a shower of bullets.

Three men came tumbling down over the wall to safety; one crawled over to Benjamin, near out of breath. "Your brother in-law—Nathaniel (Southworth)—he was killed. I saw him fall."

Benjamin felt his body shake. He stared at the ground. Instantly he wondered what he was going to say to his wife and to all her family. *Nathaniel was entrusted to me. He was just twenty-seven.* But before he had another moment to think, a flash caught the corner of his eye. He turned to take a look.

Nathaniel popped up from among the peas, very much alive. He clapped a bullet in the forehead of a native that was running straight at him, hatchet raised. Then he spun around and ran the rest of the way to the wall, flopped over it to safety, breathing hard, unhurt, and rather pleased with himself.

Benjamin studied him a moment and breathed a sigh relief.

The men were now all safe behind their little wall. Benjamin stuck his head up to spy out the enemy, as shots kept flying at them without ceasing. The smoke of the native's guns was all that betrayed their positions, and he could see that they were in possession of every rock, stump, tree, or fence; a group was inside the ruins of an old stone house above them, firing out through the windows.

He realized then that the little powder they had was all that was keeping them alive. He instructed his men to use it sparingly. "Be sure of every shot!" He then instructed them to heap up stones to raise and reinforce their wall. The enemy's shots kept raining over them and into the sand, just beyond their feet.

At length, one of the boats came across from Sandy Point.

The natives raised their weapons and shot unrelenting at the boat. The helmsman kept his distance, just short of where the water was alive from the bullets, splashing up a storm. He would not draw any closer.

Benjamin yelled, "Send your canoe ashore!"

His men joined in the yelling.

"Come ashore, man!"

"For God's sake!"

"My ammunition is spent!"

But no amount of waving, yelling, or pleading could urge that helmsman to come in to fetch them.

Benjamin was now wise to the danger of having the enemy overhear and understand their plight. He told his men to be quiet, and yelled one more time at the ship, "Send that canoe ashore or I'll shoot you myself!"

The boat left.

Watching it leave, the enemy was emboldened. They thickened their fire unmercifully upon Benjamin and his men.

One of the younger ones, fleet of foot, talked first to his mates, then pleaded with the captain. "Let me run, sir. I am almost out of powder. We are gonna die if we stay here!"

Benjamin studied their faces, filled with anguish. "Tell me, everyone—how much powder do you have?"

"I have half a horn."

"I do too."

"I have a few shots left."

Most of the men still had some. But they were nearing the end.

Benjamin thought a moment, then addressed his men. "You have seen so far how all of us have been kept safe, out there in the field, and now here. Not a one of us has even been hit; yet we have seen many of their men fall. I tell you—this is remarkable, considering there are so many of them against so few of us." He tilted his eyes upward at the sky. "It is the wonderful providence of God that has preserved us." He again looked at his men and smiled with confidence. "I tell you, if you will be patient, if you will be prudent with your ammunition, use it sparingly, that I believe that God will preserve us; and not a hair on any one of your heads will fall to the ground."

The men studied Benjamin, seeing his resolve.

"Are you with me?"

They nodded.

"Good then." He looked at the last of his army at the end of the wall, a teenager. He pointed. "You, there. Pick up that stone and set it there."

The boy hesitated, then lifted the flat stone up on its end like a shield; he raised it into place atop the wall. At that moment a bullet exploded with full force against the other side of the stone, a bullet that otherwise would surely have hit him in the head. He let go of the stone, and fell flat to the ground.

Benjamin crawled over to the boy and placed his hand on him. "Are you hurt, son?"

The boy was shaking. He looked up. "N-no, sir." He studied his fingers, just to be sure. "It—it missed me."

"See now, how God has kept you safe?" Benjamin looked back down the line at everyone. "How about we put up some more stones?"

The group earnestly set about to raising up their barricade.

The sun was descending over Aquidneck Island. The woods now echoed with a constant yelling and shouting of the enemy, every bit of three hundred men. Evening was coming.

Lake spied a sloop upriver, near Gold Island, about five miles distant. A cool wind was blowing out of the northwest, hurrying the small craft in their direction. He pointed it out to the captain.

The sloop looked familiar to Benjamin. He studied it as it drew near, then called out across the surface of the water. "Is that you, Roger?!" He suspected it belonged to his neighbor, Captain Roger Golding.

A moment later, the cry drifted back, *"Benjamin?!"*

A smile formed on Benjamin's face. "Hey there. We sure could use a ride." Benjamin's confidence was blooming, for he knew Roger to be a fearless and trustworthy friend.

Golding tossed out his anchor and pulled down his sails. Now a hail of bullets flew in the direction of his sloop, tearing through the sails and colors, splintering the boards at the stern. Undeterred, he let out his canoe on a cable; it was drawn along by the wind and current toward their position on shore.

Benjamin turned to his men. He directed them to fire at the enemy for cover, while sending two at a time to run down to the water to climb into the canoe and be pulled away. Once they had boarded the sloop, the process repeated, ferrying two more. As they escaped, the enemy kept them under constant fire, while Benjamin's men on the shore, and now out on the boat, returned their shots. Every native that stepped out to come closer was cut down by one of their sure shots.

At last it was Benjamin's turn to leave, with everyone else safe onboard. But before he picked up to run, he spied his hat and cutlass some twenty yards past the end of the wall, where he had dropped them on his way down. He couldn't imagine leaving behind a perfectly good hat and sword for the enemy. He charged his gun with the last of his powder, the poor amount that it was, and ran out from cover, brandishing his weapon toward the enemy. He picked up the items, turned and ran toward the canoe, then fired his last shot, watching as the ball carried just halfway there and fell into the sand.

Two bullets struck the canoe as he leaped into it, another knocked his hat off; one more stuck into a slender post in the aft, positioned directly in front of his heart.

Now bobbing along in the current, Benjamin turned and peeked over the gunnels. He watched as the sloop weighed anchor and raised its sail, pulling fast away from the shore, and seeing all fourteen of his men on board straining together, tugging on the cable with a singularity of purpose, towing him in to safety.

13

Arriving back at the Mount Hope garrison, Benjamin was reunited with Fuller, learning that his group had also come under attack. Due to the size of the native force assailing them, Fuller's men had fled to the remnants of an old stone house. From there they fired sparingly out of the windows and into the thickets where their assailants hid themselves. As the day wore on, the number of Indians swelled, tirelessly taking shots at any crack and crevice in the structure. Inside, the men huddled in fear, as the bullets ricocheted around. Surprisingly, no bullet hit anyone directly, but the flying bits of lead and splinters of stone kept the men in a constant state of alarm. Fuller was grateful that the structure had not been made of wood, and that the roof was long gone, or surely they would have been set on fire. Finally, after six long hours, a boat arrived to ferry them to safety. The men ran from the house, splashing out into the river under a hail of fire. Two were shot as they ran, yet managed to escape. The rest got away unhurt, but their spirits had been shattered.

Two days later, Benjamin went on reconnaissance back to Aquidneck Island and to seek provision for the army in his official role as commissary general. There, he met with

John Alderman, an Indian who had recently come over from Pocasset with his family, having deserted Weetamoo to seek sanctuary among the English, and having brought with him a group of other natives, just as Benjamin had advised— Benjamin knew the man, having met with him several times before. Alderman and his friends gave an account of the state of the Indians and described the locations of Weetamoo's many camps where she might be found. Several of them offered to accompany Benjamin as his pilot.

Armed with this intelligence, Benjamin returned to the Mount Hope garrison. There, Major Cudworth expressed his readiness to support a foray into Pocasset to search for the enemy, or to weaken them by breaking off more disaffected natives.

Eighteen of the ablest soldiers from Captain Daniel Henchman's company were drawn off, equipped, and dispatched under the command of their lieutenant, then placed under Benjamin. Several in the group had been with Benjamin at the peas field battle and were anxious for the opportunity to serve under him again. Then having marched two miles south to Mount Cove, at the foot of Mount Hope, and before they had a chance to board a ferry, they were intercepted by a courier with an order from high command to halt, to wait there for further instruction.

A half hour later, the commander in chief, Major Bradford, arrived on horseback. He had not been present at the garrison the whole time Benjamin had been there reporting of the opportunity. Thus Benjamin presumed that Bradford merely wanted to hear directly of their plans and to wish them well before they departed on their excursion.

Bradford dismounted as in a hurry. He waved Benjamin and his lieutenant aside to speak with them privately.

Benjamin studied the machinations on the Major's face as he explained his plan. He could see it was about to be withdrawn.

Bradford shook his head. "But how do you know that Philip and all his men are not now at Weetamoo's camp? Or that the rest of Weetamoo's men have not returned to join her?"

"I have good intelligence from Alderman. I know the man well. He can be trusted—as can his friends who have shown their trust in us by departing from Weetamoo."

"I have no trust of anyone who has been with Weetamoo."

Benjamin recognized the squaw sachem's reputation among the English, since her first husband had been Alexander (Wamsutta), the deceased brother of Philip. By being part of the inner circle of Philip's family, she was most distrusted.

"How could you possibly know if the enemy has not all come together and are not now laying for you in ambush?"

Benjamin's eyes widened. He re-gathered his thoughts. "I have no reason to doubt Alderman or to be discouraged by his report. And I have confidence that his men can lead us to the spot where we might encourage her to go to the Island with the rest of her people, to escape the war." He glanced at his lieutenant and straightened. "We are willing to hazard the brunt."

"The enemy's number is so great. And you do not know now how many more of their numbers have been added." Bradford turned and looked across at Benjamin's men. "And your company is so small. It is not practical for you to face them, or to risk falling under attack." He focused on Benjamin with resolve. "And even if you could possibly kill all of those that come against you, I could not accept losing a single life of one of your men."

Benjamin felt his inertia slipping. He peered over across the bay at Aquidneck Island, then pointed to the top of the hill there. "Then I would ask, sir, please lead a large company of men to that windmill. There, on that high ground, they will be out of danger, and they will be in position to better supply our expedition."

The major studied Benjamin as he finished making his case. At last he placed his hand on Benjamin's shoulder. "Come back with me to the garrison, where we might further discuss this plan, and where we might equip you with more men. This is too weighty a matter to proceed without first considering proper advice."

Benjamin felt his frustration welling. Yet he was in no position to question orders from his superior. He smiled and nodded. "Yes sir."

Benjamin tried to contain his disappointment as he and his men returned to the Mount Hope garrison; home now to what he privately said was "the losing fort." He would have to continue to wait for his chance.

14

While Benjamin and his men waited at the garrison, reports kept filtering in, telling of the violence and destruction that had happened in Taunton, giving details of the number killed and houses burned. Then came word that Middleborough and Dartmouth in Plymouth County had both been burned to the ground, and that men, women, and children had been dragged from their houses and slain, stripped naked, and left lying in their fields. And if this had not been horrible enough, it was told how the Indians had flayed the skin off the victims' faces and heads, leaving behind an unrecognizable, yet unforgettable sight to those who had to bring dignity to the disposal of the remains. Fear took a stranglehold on the Confederated Colonies.

Then came word of a different sort, that men of the Massachusetts militia had ventured into the territory of the Narragansetts, on the mainland, west of Aquidneck, and had there signed a peace treaty with the natives there, being additionally assured of their aid in the English plan to destroy Philip and all his adherents. A wave of relief swept the garrison, since the English bore no little concern over the vast number and ferocious reputation of these near-

111

neighbors, who otherwise could easily have sided with Philip in the rebellion and swept them all away.

At last, two more companies, sixty men, were raised and assigned to Benjamin's plan, one led by Captain Thomas Baxter, the other by Captain John Hunter, a Praying Indian of the Nipmuc tribe. Together they boarded a sloop that ferried them across the bay to the mainland at Fall River. With one of Alderman's friends accompanying them as their pilot, they marched in search of Weetamoo.

They had traveled barely a quarter-mile east into the woods when they startled three natives at their campsite, who took fire at them, missed, then turned to run. Captain Hunter took aim and fired, striking one of them in the knee, knocking him to the ground; the other two got away. Hunter and Benjamin ran up to the Indian, intent to question him.

The native peered up at Captain Hunter; his shoulders, nose, and forehead were covered in black paint. "Hello, John."

Hunter started. He studied the man's eyes. "David?"

The native nodded as he grabbed his knee; his face curled in pain.

Hunter turned to Benjamin. "He is my cousin. And he was with me before, with John Eliot" (Eliot was the well-known English missionary). He sighed, then turned back to the native. "How long have you been with Philip?"

David squeezed his wound to try and stave the bleeding. "I suppose—a month." He thought a moment. "I was with him in Taunton."

"Taunton?" Hunter shook his head in disgust. "How? How could you?"

David stared at his knee, then lifted his hand, now drenched in blood. He looked up at Benjamin, then at his cousin. "John, I—I killed a man—and his family."

Hunter and Benjamin looked at each other.

"I don't know why I did it. I—I just joined in with the others. It—it seemed so—so easy."

Hunter said nothing.

David again stared at his blood. He took a deep breath and let it out slowly. "I hope you will be able to find Mary, and save her." He looked up at both men. "My squaw, she is innocent. Please do not hold her to blame on account of me."

Hunter nodded. "I will do all I can for her."

David studied his leg, then appealed to Benjamin. "I cannot walk. I understand what I deserve. I desire no favor for me. You will have to finish me here." He glanced across at his possessions, left by the campfire. "But I would like to have a whiff of tobacco."

Hunter retrieved his pipe, still lit. He handed it to him.

David took a long draw and closed his eyes.

Hunter stepped behind the native, pulled his hatchet from his belt and stared at Benjamin. He made his decision. With one swift blow to the back of his head, he dispatched his cousin.

At that moment, shots were heard in the woods nearby, followed by shouting. Benjamin ran off to see what was happening.

Farther ahead, they came into the center of Weetamoo's camp, with all the fires still burning.

Benjamin looked around. A group of his men were crowded in front of one of the wigwams, restraining two natives. A third lay on the ground, dead. He approached them.

One of Benjamin's men explained. "When we came into camp, we saw this one—" he pointed at the dead man, "—running out with his gun. I shot him." Then pointing at the other two, he continued. "They said he told them he would 'kill an Englishman before he eat his dinner.'"

Benjamin stepped over to the wigwam, bent, and peered inside. A fire was yet blazing, with a piece of meat roasting above it on a spit. Benjamin withdrew his head, straightened, and looked all around the camp. He estimated there were more than a hundred wigwams, now empty.

"They all ran away, except for these three. The others must have heard us approach and fled—in that direction." He pointed to the far end of the camp.

Leaving a few men behind to guard their rear, and to hold the prisoners, Benjamin and his men moved in fast pursuit to the far end of the camp. There they entered a cedar swamp, spreading themselves out to form a front, looking for clues to ascertain the direction of the enemy. The way proved thick and boggy, and the men sank in to their waists, which greatly slowed their progress.

Now fearful and watching for any sign of the enemy, the men shot at anything that moved. More than once, they saw a bush stir, fired, and then learned that they had struck and injured one of their own men.

After an hour, and now with daylight fading, Benjamin ordered all his men to his left and right to stop and stay silent, standing still in the slime.

Directly ahead, past the thick underbrush, they could hear the cries of women and children.

Far off to the right, the sound of gunfire erupted. Baxter's men were in that direction.

All in one moment, the bushes ahead seemed to move. Without any command, several of Benjamin's men discharged their weapons.

The bushes responded, firing back, then rushed at them with hatchets raised; for the natives had camouflaged themselves by strapping green boughs to their chests. And now the whole of the swamp came alive, ringing out against them with the terrible sound of whoops and cries.

Benjamin's men emptied their guns.

A dozen of the enemy went down; the rest, more than a hundred, kept on coming.

"RUN!" yelled Benjamin.

The whole of the English turned and fled, rushing frustrated through the mire, staying but paces ahead of their enemy, with their guns emptied, urged along by panic.

At the edge of the swamp, they re-entered the native camp, kicked off the slime, and darted through the woods, racing back to their sloop, with a line of natives firing at their heels.

Carrying their wounded, they retreated to their vessel and shoved off in haste, away from the hail of bullets coming at them from the trees, hearing all the while the screams that sounded worse to them than loss—yet to their enemy's ears, more surely was the great cry of victory.

Benjamin and his men returned again to the losing fort.

15

Back at the fort and recovering from their wounds, the talk was all about the death and destruction at Dartmouth. In response, the high command summoned most of Plymouth's forces to go to Dartmouth's relief. Benjamin and his men went along.

At sunrise, two hundred Englishmen boarded a small fleet of sloops moored at Mount Cove, then set sail south, working their way out of the mouth of Narragansett Bay. At Newport, they turned their course to the east, and now with the wind at their backs, they passed by Sakonnet and entered into Buzzards Bay. Late in the day, they came to a small cove and steered north, into the mouth of the Apponagansett River. Ahead, on the east bank, lay Russell's garrison, a stone house surrounded by a wooden palisade, still standing firm, alive with campfires burning. English guards waved happily at them from their towers as they moored at the dock. Seeing now the fort intact, Benjamin's concerns were greatly eased; for none had known what to expect, whether there would be any citizens left alive there.

As they came ashore and approached the stockade, Benjamin and the other captains were greeted by Ralph Earl, a leader of the local citizens. He ran down to meet them and gave them a fast report of their situation. "We have taken in many natives who have just now surrendered themselves. I am glad to say the conflict is over." He escorted the captains up to the top of the bank and forward to the gate.

Inside, the stockade was filled with natives: men, women, and children. Intermingled with them were what remained of the local citizenry, everyone surprisingly at ease. Members of the local militia stood by, not even holding their weapons.

Ralph pointed at one of the militia, "And here is our captain, Samuel Eels." They approached him and introduced themselves.

Benjamin studied the natives. He did not immediately recognize any of them. He faced Eels, eyes narrowed. "Why did they surrender?"

Eels placed his hand on Earl's shoulder. "Ralph here, he has been living in peace among these natives for years. He persuaded one of his neighbors, a friendly Indian, who was with us here in the garrison—that man, over there." Eels pointed. "He persuaded him to go out and speak with his brothers, to bid them to lay down their guns and to come and be with us, here inside, that we might no longer be killing one another. We promised them sanctuary and protection from Philip."

Again Benjamin studied the crowd. Several of the English women were seen handing out food to the natives, who were seated around the campfires, together engaged in pleasant conversations. It was hard to imagine the two sides had the day before been shooting at each other. He smiled and looked at Eels, unexpectedly wondering what had become of his own purpose in coming there. "So, how can we help you?"

118

Eels reflected. "We have many dead. Some have been lying in the fields for days." His face darkened. "We have not felt safe to leave here before today. They need a Christian burial. And I could not suffer these people to go out to see their loved ones in such a sorry state."

Benjamin glanced at his fellow captains with sympathetic eyes. They nodded. "We will take care of them." Then aware of his role as commissary general, he changed the subject. "I do not see how you will be able much longer to feed these natives, let alone yourselves."

Earl interjected, "I count one-hundred-twelve. And I was hoping we could direct them to Plymouth for supply."

"Yes. We can take them there in safety."

Benjamin and his fellow captains met that evening and divided their force. The next morning, thirty of the militia accompanied Ralph Earl and the native contingent on a march of forty miles north and east to Plymouth. In the meantime, Benjamin and the rest of the army went out into the countryside and gathered up the dead, burying the remains where they lay.

Two weeks later, their task complete, and feeling confidence rising at Russell's Garrison, Benjamin and his militia returned to Mount Hope.

16

When Benjamin and his men arrived back at the fort, they found the place a-flood with stories of events that had taken place while they had been away in Dartmouth. He and three other captains were summoned to a meeting with Major Cudworth to be properly briefed. It was evening when they entered into the commander's tent. Cudworth rose from behind his desk, greeted them, and asked his officers to be seated.

After giving each of them a chance to recount news of their visit to Dartmouth, he began, "Shortly after you left, on the 19th, I ordered Captain Henchman and his Massachusetts men and the Providence men under Captain Edmonds, together with the Plymouth militia, to cross the bay over to Pocasset." He looked directly at Benjamin, "We were relying on the intelligence you gave us regarding the location of Weetamoo and Philip."

Benjamin nodded.

"The entire contingent marched directly into the swamp and came upon a native village of about one hundred wigwams. Unfortunately, the Indians had heard our coming

121

and were ready. They fired upon our army, killing eight and wounding two dozen of our men.

"Undeterred, Edmonds returned fire, and slew more than a dozen of the Indians, before the rest turned and fled into the swamp, taking with them their women and children.

"Our militias wasted no time and followed them into the swamp.

"Now this is, as you know, Benjamin, a very thick swamp, lush with greenery, and one that is very familiar to the Indians. And while we did our best to follow their tracks, we had several mishaps, shooting at shaking bushes only to learn that we had fired upon our own men.

"As the day grew late, and it became apparent that we were in unfamiliar territory, Captain Henchman made the decision to pull back, not risking any further the safety of his men. So he ordered a retreat. After all, we had roused the enemy from their homes, fleeing without their food stocks, and we could readily wait for them outside of the swamp, enjoying our ample supplies."

One of the captains interjected, "You would starve them out."

"Precisely." Cudworth smiled.

By now, Benjamin was squirming, for it seemed to him that yet another opportunity to force Philip to surrender had been missed, a good opportunity because he would surely have been slowed and burdened by having all his army's women and children in tow. But he would wait to hear the rest of the story. He stayed silent.

"Then when our men had returned from the swamp, I ordered the construction of a new fort, that we might hold that position and block Philip's return—keep him contained in the swamp."

Benjamin screamed silently to himself, *Wasting initiative on another fort!* He shifted his weight in his chair and leaned on his fist, trying to restrain his anger.

"I named it 'Fort Leverett.'" Cudworth smiled, pleased with himself, that he had honored the governor of the Massachusetts Bay. One at a time, he examined the faces of his captains, looking for their approval. When his eyes at last fell on Benjamin's face, seeing his jaw set, and recalling what his captain had said about the Mount Hope fort; he refocused on his report. "I ordered Henchman to construct the fort and to man it. And seeing that we no longer needed such a large force to hold the position, I allowed the Massachusetts men to return to their homes to tend to their farms. Major Savage and Mosley departed from here, and Captain Prentice was ordered to march from here on Mendon, which we had learned had fallen under attack by the Nipmucs."

Just then a courier came to the door of the tent, wearing a face of urgency. He interrupted the meeting. "Major Cudworth, sir. I have an express for you." He strode into the tent and handed him the note.

Cudworth unfolded the note and tilted it toward the candle, studying the words.

The men watched as his face turned white.

"What is it, sir?" asked one of the captains.

Cudworth handed the note to him.

He read it silently, then handed it along.

The note came at last to Benjamin. He studied the words:

Late last night, August 1st, at low tide, Philip and all his men waded over to the far side of the Taunton River, taking with them their women and children on rafts. They escaped to the north.

—Capt. Daniel Henchman

Benjamin folded the note and handed it back to the major, looking downward, avoiding eye contact. He knew of no better way to conceal his utter frustration.

17

Benjamin left Mount Hope to go home to Duxbury, returning like so many of the colonial militiamen to his farm. But he was not motivated to leave the war for the same reason as the other men, to tend to family; he was leaving out of utter frustration with the hapless leadership and weak decisions, decisions that had allowed bad will and criminal behavior of a few to escalate out of control.

On his way home, Benjamin veered off and traveled through Plymouth, curious to know if there was any other news. Near midday, he crested the hill on West Street and descended into the village. That was when the distant disturbance first fell on his ears, a faraway groaning. He stopped and listened carefully. It sounded like many cries of human despair. He set off toward the sound, driven now to comprehend its source and reason.

At the village center, he turned south, toward the courthouse, hearing the roar increase. Ahead, a crowd of village folk was seen quietly and solemnly dispersing from the courthouse. Now closer toward the sound, he looked to his left and saw it, hundreds of men—soldiers—pressing inward against a turbulent crowd. At the center of the humanity was the active skirmish, the core of the cries, the wailing of scores of native men, women, and children, swirling together in the midst of a savage clash, pressed along against their will by the English militia, for they were being moved, moved downward to the harbor.

Benjamin drew to a halt and studied the brawl. As he sat high in the saddle, a man ran up to him, waving and calling out his name. It was Ralph Earl.

Earl spoke in desperation, short of breath. "They just adjourned—the council for war."

Benjamin dismounted. He stared at Ralph, eyes narrowed.

"It was a trial. The Indians—the natives from Dartmouth—several were identified as rifling through houses—as 'actors in the war'—*and the whole rest have been found to be compliers with Philip.*"

Benjamin stood, straight-faced.

"They have all been sold into slavery. *Now they are to be transported out of the country.*"

Benjamin went numb, as though his ears had just been shattered by an explosion. He stared at the swirling crowd, unable to reason, unable to make any sense of what he was seeing. He remembered the promises he had made. He shook himself alert. He leaned forward, toward Ralph. "But what about the promises you made to them when they surrendered? Did you not testify, did you not have a voice in the council?"

"I did. And Samuel Eels testified as well. We both said the same thing: that the natives had only surrendered on the promise that they would be allowed to return to their villages, and again live in peace." Ralph hung his head and groaned. "I gave them my word—*MY WORD.*"

Benjamin studied Ralph's face, red with anguish, his eyes filled with tears. He thought a moment and resolved what to do. He took hold of Ralph's arm. "Where is Captain Eels?"

The two men searched the crowd. They spotted Eels standing to the side, away from the fray, engaged in what looked like an argument with a dozen other captains. He was gesturing, very animated. Benjamin knew most of those men with him. He approached them with Ralph at his side.

The men stopped their discussion when they saw Benjamin approach, smiling, acting cordial, for they knew him quite well and considered him a friend. They extended their hands in a warm greeting. "Nice to see you, Benjamin."

Benjamin shook each of their hands, then turned to Eels and greeted him in the same cordial manner. From the corner of his eye, Benjamin detected the other men watching this exchange; he sensed their enmity toward Samuel.

He faced the men directly. "What is the misunderstanding here?" He watched the smiles fade from their faces, their sudden discomfort, their unwillingness to look him in the eye.

None of them replied.

"Well? What then?" he asked, pointedly.

Samuel could no longer contain himself. "They just condemned innocent women and children to a life of slavery—*for nothing!*"

"*Innocent?!*" shouted one of them. "*Do you call feeding Philip's army, keeping his place a secret—do you call that nothing?*"

Others joined in the shouting.

"*And burning property?*"

"*And stealing cattle?*"

"*Is that innocent?!*"

"*Is that nothing?*"

"*We were too kind to them. They should all instead be hanged!*"

127

Benjamin could hardly believe what he was hearing. The shouting escalated. Eels and Earl leaned forward at the men and shouted back. The two sides grabbed at one another, making ready to fight.

Benjamin raised both hands and shouted, *"Gentlemen!"* He forced himself between them, pushing them apart. He studied the faces of his Plymouth friends, then turned to Eels and Earl. *"Enough."* He measured his words. "Surely this is a misunderstanding. We should not rush to justice. Surely we can examine the evidence and revisit this decision."

The Plymouth men recoiled from Benjamin, wide-eyed. "You are not siding with *them*—are you?"

Benjamin's jaw dropped. He uttered, "Them?"

"Yes—you—*them*—" pointing at Eels and Earl, "and all the other Indian lovers—*the savage beasts!*"

Earl again exploded. "They are *not* savages! They are my neighbors."

Benjamin watched the argument erupt afresh, seeing the men hurl insults at one another. His mind raced, seeking after wisdom, searching out some proper word that would restore peace. Again, he raised his voice above the fray. *"There is guilt enough from both sides!* I have come from the battle. I have seen the anger of both sides. And I have seen the bodies lying *dead* in the field—the bodies of *both* sides—the men, the women, the children. Let us not rage against each other like they did." He waited as they became quiet. He took a breath, measured his thoughts, and continued, "I cannot rightly declare to God that every Indian is innocent. Neither can any one of you face God and declare rightly to him that every Indian is guilty."

The men squirmed.

"But I will tell you this, gentlemen. This is hateful what was done, to sell them as slaves—*hateful!* If—if we wish to contain this violence, and if we are serious about ending this conflict—*before it spreads to all of New England*—then we must forgive and forget. For when the rest of the native nation sees how we treated these few, there will never again be peace. We must right this wrong."

One of the Plymouth men who had been silent raised his head to speak. "You have had your say, Benjamin. And I have listened. But now I will tell you what I know. *My* house, *my* barns—they were burned to the ground by *the beasts*. A-and my wife, *my sons*—" He became distraught and could no longer speak.

Another Plymouth man gathered his friend in his arms and looked across at Benjamin. "William's family—they were massacred by the savage wretches."

A third stepped forward and stared at Benjamin, his jaw set. "I cannot *forget* the evil. And though God be my judge, I also cannot *forgive*." Pointing at Eels and Earl, he continued, "—and you, Benjamin—you and your friends here—you are on the *wrong* side. There must be justice."

Benjamin glanced silently at Eels and Earl. He felt helpless against the hatred. What more could he say?

The argument was over. One at a time, the Plymouth men turned and walked away, each man wearing a look of disgust.

Benjamin saw it clearly now. There could be no peace.

18

To Benjamin it seemed that the remainder of the summer
was spent by the militias in providing for the forts, and
maintaining the forces there, while Philip ran off across the
Rehoboth plain, crossing the Pawtuxet River, racing more
than a hundred miles into the county, first to the north, then
west toward Albany. Along the way, Philip aligned himself
with the Nipmucs and the Nashaus, and together they left
behind a swath of death and devastation, burned houses and
towns—first Mendon, then Brookfield, then Deerfield, and
on to Northfield before turning west and reaping destruction
in Springfield, then Hatfield, and gathering more allies in
the Pocumtucs and mighty Narragansetts. In the meantime,
in the eastern provinces, hundreds of Abenakis were
sympathetic to the mayhem and joined in, setting every
village east of Saco to flames, including Scarborough,
Falmouth, and Kennebec, and leaving the few English
survivors there short of supplies and ammunition. Each of
these battles took its toll upon the English militia. Captains
Hutchinson, Wheeler, Beers and Lothrop all lost their lives.
All thirty-six of Beers' men died with him. Seventy-six died
with Lothrop under the assault of seven hundred Indians in

131

Deerfield, a massacre that came to be known as Bloody Brook—the color of the little stream that ran out from village that day. And not just soldiers were killed in these clashes, settlers' farms were the common target, and those killed included women and children, pulled from their beds, slaughtered and, in an act of deliberate humiliation, left lying naked in the fields, where they became food for wild animals.

While all this devastation was taking place, Benjamin tried to focus on anything but the war, staying in the comfort of his home in Duxbury, occupied with the daily routine of farm chores but ever distracted by the constant drip of horrid news. Each report drew him back to the memories of one poor decision after another that had allowed a small spark in southeast Massachusetts in June to explode into all of New England now in flames. *Would that it had been snuffed out so easily at the beginning.* He buried his head into his chores to try and forget.

On October 27th, Benjamin appeared in Plymouth court. He had been summoned there concerning a debt he owed to a friend, Richard Beers, who had recently been killed in the defense of Northfield. Benjamin sat before the jury and magistrate and listened to the testimony of Richard French, the executor of Beers' estate.

To Benjamin, the suit was entirely unnecessary, unnecessary because he had every intention to pay the full amount of his debt, the sum of forty shillings. But this was the process of the court, to care for the heirs, and he acceded to the court's decision.

When the proceeding was over, Benjamin paid French, then turned and looked out at the near-empty chamber. A woman stood there in a dark dress, a black cap on her head, with two neatly attired young men at her side. Her eyes were fixed on Benjamin. It was Beers' widow, apparently waiting to speak with him. He approached.

"Elizabeth," he said as he took her hand in both of his. He spoke softly, "I am so sorry to be seeing you under these circumstances." He shook hands with her two sons. "Eleazer…and Jabez." Benjamin quietly looked at them, searching for the right words to comfort them. At last he spoke, "I am—I am so sorry for your loss." He felt himself losing control of his emotions.

"Thank you." She looked proudly at her sons. "My boys—I mean, my men—they are helping. God made us a family for a reason."

He forced a smile. "Yes." he said, then turned away and stared unseeing into the corner of the room, trying to imagine what next to say. He surely couldn't mention Richard's service in the war, for standing right before him was a family bereft of a husband and father—the very proof of how pointless his service had been. No. He would not say anything to discourage them, neither would he disparage the war. Those thoughts were off limits to share with others. He nodded at them and quietly walked out of the courtroom.

At home, he told his wife Alice of the interchange with the Beers, for she was his confidant in all matters.

For months she had listened to his ramblings, his ever-present regrets over the war. She had let those talks of his play out without comment, without pushing back, not prying, allowing him to empty his heart. But today was different. She spoke at last, "Richard was a good friend."

He welcomed her voice. "Yes. Yes, indeed."

She measured him, and pressed in. "He was so often thinking of others before himself. That was why he served."

He stiffened. "But it—it was such a waste."

Alice stepped up close and took hold of his arms, looking him in the eyes. "He knew what he was getting into. I must disagree. No. His death was not a waste."

He shook his head. "No. You do not know what I have seen—the murder, the destruction—and it was all so, so *unnecessary.*"

"You cannot say that." She backed away. "There is nothing in life that is unnecessary. To everything there is a season—and a time to every purpose under heaven."

Benjamin looked away.

Again she drew close and touched his face, turning it back to her. "Man may waste his life, but God wastes nothing."

He studied her eyes, admiring her strength.

"I know you. It is eating you up inside. You want to go back. And I think you should. Yes, I love having you here with us; these months together have been so good. But they need you. They need you back."

He pulled her close to him. He knew she was right.

Part Two

19

When the Narragansetts were found to have some of Beers' weapons, it was certain that they'd been aiding Philip's men, women, and children. On November 12th, the war commissioners of the Confederated Colonies had written to Boston:

> "We find that the Narragansetts, under pretense of friendship and false and perfidious holding as is reported to us, have made great correspondence with the enemy and have been in more open hostility receiving, relieving, and, contrary to their covenant, detaining many of the enemy men, women, and children to their great advantage and our prejudice, and by many other insolvencies have been declaring their enmity for us since they are willing participants in the war against us. We resolve to raise a new army of 1,000 men in the following proportions: 527 Massachusetts, 158 Plymouth, and 115 Connecticut; and hope, by the providence of God, to reduce them to reason."

The combined army was placed under the command of Governor Josiah Winslow, who bore the rank of general. The Massachusetts troops were placed under Major Appleton with Captains Mosley, Gardner, Davenport, Oliver, Johnson, and Prentice; Plymouth was under Major Bradford and Captain Gorham; and Connecticut was under Major Treat with Captains Seeley, Gallup, Mason, Watts, and Marshall.

When Benjamin heard the call for recruits, he rode to Plymouth to have an audience with Governor Winslow, who offered to assign a company of men to him. But Benjamin declined the commission, preferring instead to serve in the general's guard as a "reformado" (a reform officer), that he might gain experience to succeed to a higher rank.

On December 8th, Benjamin rode with Winslow and the Plymouth forces to Boston where they became part of a combined army of some 1500 men, including 1148 from the three colonies, additional recruits from Rhode Island, and a great number of friendly Indians. From there they marched toward Narragansett territory on the mainland, west of Aquidneck Island (Rhode Island).

Along the way, the general discoursed with Benjamin concerning their purpose to surprise Pumham, a certain Narragansett sachem and chief proponent in the war. Pumham had learned of their offensive and fled into the wilderness from his village near Warwick. And when the army reached Rehoboth on the morning of the 11th, Winslow instructed Benjamin to proceed by ferry ahead of the main force to obtain some intelligence as to the enemy's position. The army was to continue its march west and south over land.

Benjamin took with him Richard Smith, Jr., who had a blockhouse in Wickford and was well acquainted with the Narragansett territory. The two departed immediately for

Mount Hope, boarded a southbound ferry to Newport, then sailed north and west across the bay under a fair wind, arriving at Smith's Garrison in the early evening.

Wasting no time, Benjamin began to inquire of the enemy's resorts, wigwams, and sleeping places. Then taking with him a half-dozen men, he set off on a march to the north, toward Warwick.

The night was cold, but the little band was blessed with the light of the moon. Before daybreak, they fell upon a native village and captured eighteen Narragansetts, with the purpose to present these to General Winslow when he arrived.

The Massachusetts and Plymouth troops arrived at Smith's Garrison the next evening, Sunday the 12th, with Winslow and the rest of his guard. Benjamin explained their exploits to the general and showed him the captives.

Winslow looked over the natives. "I presume they have not told you where the enemy is hiding."

Benjamin shook his head.

"Still, I appreciate your actions in bringing them in. We will send a couple to Boston for questioning." The general smiled at Benjamin. "I have no doubt that, with your faculty, you will supply us with many more captives before the war is over."

That evening the army camped in Smith's yard, all around his blockhouse. Overnight came the first snowfall of the season, a sudden and powerful storm, which continued the whole of the next day. The entire army huddled in their tents in blizzard conditions, as the storm buried them in more than two feet of snow. Meanwhile, having no other firewood, members of the army pulled apart Smith's wooden fences to burn for warmth. To feed the hungry army, Smith found himself unexpectedly supplying their need, offering up animals from his herd of cattle, goats, and hogs. A dozen livestock were butchered and cooked each day of their stay there.

The next day, the skies finally cleared. Winslow sent two companies of men out on forays in search of enemy positions, hoping also to find the rest of the English Army, who had not yet arrived at the garrison. One of the companies raided a Narragansett village and killed nine Indians, captured twelve, and burned 150 wigwams.

On Wednesday, a scouting party went out again and found the frozen remains of several stragglers who had been cut off from the rest of the army. They brought the bodies back to Smith's garrison and buried them in a corner of his lot. More snow fell that afternoon, evening, and then on into the next morning.

On Thursday, Captain Prentice led his troop of horsemen some ten miles south to Bull's Garrison in Pettaquamscut. They returned with the news that the Indians had burned the place and killed fifteen English men, women, and children. Prentice's men captured a Narragansett man there and brought him back, an Indian named Peter.

Peter had a trove of information and he was willing to share it. He was called into a meeting with General Winslow and his guard. There he made his disaffection known for his tribal leaders; he was disgusted with the war and the destruction he saw already falling on his own people. He promised to guide them to the native hiding place, describing its situation and construction in great detail. Benjamin smiled, knowing that at last the high command had the information they needed.

The next morning, Friday December 17th, Major Treat and his captains led the Connecticut army, together with 150 Mohegan natives, south to Bull's Garrison to set up base camp. On Saturday, the Plymouth, Rhode Island, and

Massachusetts troops joined them there at 5:00 p.m., having trudged all day through the third snowfall of the week. Overnight, a strong north wind blew through their camp; the skies cleared, and the temperature plunged.

Before the break of day, the men awoke and assembled in formation, first the troops from Massachusetts, then Plymouth and Rhode Island, with Connecticut and the Mohegans at the rear. Then with the frozen pink sky dawning at their backs, they marched out from the ruins of the garrison, westward through the deep snow, with Captain Mosley at the head of the column and Peter the Indian beside him, now resting on their plan to surprise and overwhelm the whole company of the enemy.

20

Benjamin had had a hard time sleeping, but not just because of the extreme cold. He knew that the army would be marching out the next day on the first serious assault of the war, and that they would be heading into battle without him. The thought of being out of the heat of action, while his friends bore the brunt of it, had been simply too much to bear. He had wrestled with his feelings all night long.

The next morning, after the main force had left toward the objective, the generals' guard and a protection force of two hundred men remained behind at Bull's Garrison. By the time these had departed, they were two hours behind.

Riding out beside Winslow, Benjamin at last yielded to his impatience. He turned to the general. "Sir, I request your leave, that I might ride on ahead and join the main force."

Winslow looked across at him, brows raised.

"I want to be able to assist my friends in battle."

The general shook his head. "We have already discussed the plan and made our decision."

"I could hardly sleep last night, sir—the thought that I would be missing the action."

"No, Captain. I need you here in my guard."

Benjamin stared down at his hands. "Sir. I'm not doing you any good here, riding along beside you. You have two hundred other men here guarding you. I could do you a lot more good by being another set of eyes up in the action." He stared at the governor's face.

Winslow's brow raised. He thought a moment. "I can see, Captain, that you are not going to stop hounding me about this."

"No, sir, uh, respectfully."

The governor nodded. "All right then. But you need to see if there is anyone who wants to go with you. You shall need a small company. I will not send you ahead alone."

Benjamin smiled. "Thank you, sir." He spun around and rode down the line of those following. In a few minutes he had raised thirty men. Then bidding his farewell to General Winslow, they set off directly.

Benjamin and his band followed the trail of the main force; it was a wide track in the deep snow, impossible to miss. Just after noon they arrived at their objective.

Benjamin motioned for silence as they dismounted and he examined the scene. With a blanket of snow covering everything, a hush fell over them, a depth of silence that defied logic, for their army of more than twelve-hundred Englishmen was somewhere about that very spot, presumably engaged in conflict with a large native force; yet not a sound could be heard. The silence was foreboding.

Where they stood, the tree line abruptly ended and the ground dropped steeply down to a small stream, now frozen solid and blanketed with virgin snow. On the far bank of the little waterway, the ground ran away several hundred feet, then rose up a few yards to a wide wall of thickets flocked with snow. The wall curved to the left and to the right, encompassing an island of several acres of upland, an island situated in the midst of the vast frozen swamp. Over and to their right, a large tree had fallen across the stream, lying like a bridge between the forest and the island. The stump was there. The tree had been felled. This was indeed the Indian fort, for it was just as Peter had described it. The track left by the English army veered to the right and led straight to the tree.

Benjamin motioned for his men to remain quiet as they left their horses and crept up to the bridge, the single point of entry to the fort. He studied the wide trunk, seeing the footprints continue across it and into the fort. There were many other footprints behind him, at the stump of the tree, aimed in the opposite direction, leading north through the woods on the right of the swamp.

He climbed up onto the bridge to gain a vantage into the fort. He saw no movement. He turned back and studied the faces of his men, then made his decision. They followed him single file across the log bridge to the other side, climbed down, and at last had their first clear view inside the fort.

Ahead was a scene of massacre; dozens of English lay dead, bodies scattered between the wigwams at the eastern end of the fort. Benjamin and his men held their hands to their faces as they stepped forward between and over them, hoping to find any among them yet alive. But all the bodies lay motionless, their blood spattered everywhere on the snow, a sickening sight. Benjamin looked at the faces of the victims; he saw several of the valiant captains had fallen with their men.

Sensing movement behind him, Benjamin gripped his gun and spun back toward the point of entry. Captain Joseph Gardner of Salem emerged from one of the wigwams and stepped toward him. But as they were looking each other in the face, there came a single report ringing from the distant trees. Gardner suddenly stopped walking and stood very still.

Benjamin studied the captain's strange expression, then saw blood running out of his eye and down his cheek. Benjamin called, "Gardner!" but got no response. He stepped close and Gardner fell forward into his arms. Benjamin lifted his hat and observed the wound. Gardner had been shot in the back of the head. He was dead.

Benjamin looked outside the fort. The shot had been fired from somewhere in the forest. He glanced quickly at the other bodies about his feet. Every one of them had been shot in the back. Seeing they were exposed, he promptly lay Gardner down, then motioned fervently to his men. They all ran with him safely back out of the fort.

On the far side of the bridge, he dispatched a courier back to the general, to explain their situation. Then they all made straight for the woods in pursuit of the sniper.

Ahead, at the edge of the tree line, they caught glimpses of a group of the enemy. Benjamin ordered his men to take careful aim and to keep firing in succession, a few shots at a time while the others reloaded.

The enemy returned fire; they discharged their weapons all at once, but to no effect, then turned and ran farther into the woods.

Now in hot pursuit, Benjamin came across a broad and bloody track left by the enemy. Following hard in the track, he caught up with one of the enemy. The native stopped, clapped his musket across his chest and turned toward Benjamin, motioning with his hand.

"Hold your fire! No one hurt him," said Benjamin to his men. He lowered his gun and stepped toward the native, hoping to gain some intelligence. But as he drew close, one of his men who had lagged behind came up and shot the Indian dead.

Benjamin turned to his man and glared.

But before he had time even to scold his soldier, there came a great shout of the enemy. It came from behind them, between them and the fort. They turned and saw many natives running from tree to tree, angling away from them and toward the fort, their guns raised. From this vantage, Benjamin and his men were hidden behind a heap of underbrush, shielded from the view of the enemy. At the same time he could see clearly through great gaps in the unfinished walls on the north side of the fort, observing the movements of the rest of the English army that now occupied it.

Benjamin waved at the fort, hoping to alert the English there as to his presence; he wanted to be sure they understood he was there, so that they might not fire upon him and his men. When that failed, he called out to a sergeant. The sergeant turned suddenly, saw him and waved.

By this time a large number of the enemy had gathered at the end of the bridge, but had dropped down out of sight. The sergeant climbed up onto the log and began stepping across, looking toward Benjamin, apparently unaware of the enemy.

Benjamin and his men rose up in one accord and made ready to fire into the enemy.

The sergeant recognized what they were doing, turned, noticed the Indians. He frantically waved his hands and yelled at Benjamin, "For God's sake! Don't shoot at them! They're our friend Indians!"

When the whole of the enemy rose up and fired at him, the sergeant realized his mistake too late. He fell over dead.

Benjamin and his company unloaded their weapons into the enemy, directly into their backs. Many fell dead; the rest rose and scattered with surprise. About a dozen ran over the log into the fort, and there climbed into a hovel made of poles, which was standing like a guardhouse at the end of the bridge.

Taking a moment to fix their cartridges, Benjamin's men were soon ready to receive his next order, which was to cross over the bridge and to overturn the hovel. They clambered up unto the tree and ran across it. Benjamin was in the lead, calling out to the English inside the fort, that they might also come and join with them in the attack. Some came running.

Benjamin ran toward the hovel, seeing that several of the enemy had found holes and had stuck the end of their guns through, now pointed directly at him. Undeterred, he called to his company, then ran on until he was struck with three bullets; one glanced off his hip. He somehow managed to keep on his feet as he discharged his gun back at the enemy.

Disabled now to go one more step, Benjamin refused his men's offers to carry him off. He instructed them instead to run on to overturn the enemy's shelter, for the Indians had just discharged all their weapons and hadn't had time to reload. But while he was urging them on, the Indians began to shoot arrows, one of which pierced through the arm of a soldier who had taken ahold of Benjamin to help him. Discouraged by the resolve of the enemy, the English drew back into the fort, and carried Benjamin with them, safely away from the fray.

By this time the English soldiers inside the fort had begun to set fire to the wigwams and houses there.

Benjamin begged them "Stop! Spare the shelters!" He could see that they were well lined and musket-proof, a good warm place to house the wounded, and they were filled with the Indian's food supplies, baskets and tubs of grain, meat, and other provisions—enough to feed the entire army until the spring. He knew all too well that that his army had no other provision, not even one biscuit left to feed all their men. He sent a courier with word to Winslow as he continued to plead with them. "Please, wait until the general arrives."

"Sorry, Mister Church. Captain Mosley told us he had orders from the general." Undeterred, they continued to burn the wigwams.

Meanwhile, Winslow approached and prepared to bring the rest of the army with him into the fort. But as he arrived at the edge of the swamp, Captain Mosley came out to meet him, wearing a look of desperation. "Sir, where are you going?"

Winslow looked down at him, his face wrinkled; yet he held back from condemning Mosley's apparent insubordination. Instead, he answered, "Into the fort."

Mosley seized hold of Winslow's horse and pleaded with him. "Sir. Your life is worth a hundred of ours. You cannot so expose yourself to the enemy's arrows."

Winslow shook his head. "Mister Church sent me word that the brunt was over, that the fort has been taken, and that we should consider it the most practical to come inside to shelter ourselves there."

Mosley bristled, for he hated Benjamin's intentions to preserve and use the enemy's shelters and provisions. "*Church has lied to you, sir. He is not in his right mind.* And if you make one more move toward the fort, I shall have to shoot your horse out from under you."

By now a doctor had come from the fort and joined with Mosley in the heat of the conversation. "Sir, Mister Church's advice will kill more of our army than the enemy has killed— for by tomorrow, the wounded will be so stiff we will not be able to move them." He stepped close. "And I have seen his own wounds, the blood flowing from his hip. If Mister Church wants to remain here, he should stanch his own wounds and bleed to death like a dog." He stood up straight.

"We need to burn this hell hole and get on back to our own garrison."

Winslow looked at the smoke of the fort now filling the sky. He studied their faces, seeing their unrelenting attitude. At last he yielded to their hatred for the enemy and their fervent disagreement with Benjamin; he gave his order.

And so the English army burned up the rest of the fort and then set off that same night to return to Smith's Garrison. And every one of them that survived that ten-hour, eighteen-mile march through the storm and bitter cold, deeply lamented their miseries as they carried with them Benjamin and all the other wounded and dying men.

21

In the weeks that followed the destruction of the Indian fort, word of the battle and its aftermath filtered throughout the Confederated Colonies. On hearing the reports, a number of the English political and spiritual leaders, anxious for any good word, declared the outcome of the "great swamp fight" a victory. But to those who had been in that fight and had seen the suffering themselves, they hardly felt victorious: sixty-eight English had been killed outright in the battle, two men were lost in the woods during the march, and another one-hundred-fifty had been wounded. And when the army returned that night to Smith's garrison at 2:00 a.m., having marched through the coldest night of the season, they could not yet rest, burdened with the immediate task to bury their dead, the bodies they had dragged with them and those who had expired along the way. Among this tally of dead, the army had lost half its senior officer corps. Of all those who had survived, four hundred were so incapacitated by exposure to the weather and lack of care that they no longer were able to serve, having become incapable of continuing in the winter campaign. Considering the graveness of their condition, had Captain Andrew

Belcher not shown up that very night at Smith's Garrison with a ship laden with provisions, there is little doubt that many more would have died. Yet despite this aid, over the next three days, fifteen more succumbed to their wounds.

Any conclusion of victory was founded on the native losses, the reports of which filtered in over the next week, losses that far eclipsed those of the English. Native survivors, those who surrendered or who had been captured, told that some seven hundred of their fighting men had been killed in battle or had died from the severe cold that followed; many fell victim to lack of food and shelter. Added to these were another three hundred native citizens dead—elderly, women, and children—most burned to death in their wigwams. These numbers amounted to one third of the Narragansett nation. This toll of death and uncounted others wounded, combined with a dwindling supply of gunpowder, drove the survivors into retreat. They had become unwilling to fight against an English army that, coincidentally, had itself become unable to continue the conflict.

Benjamin was among the six score of wounded who had been moved over to Aquidneck Island, where a clinic was hastily arranged to care for them. Benjamin had assessed his own wounds. One bullet had nearly sliced off half his thigh at the hip; the second had passed between his legs and ripped his breeches and drawers, yet only grazed his skin; and the third had pierced his hip pocket, shredding a pair of mittens he had borrowed from Captain Prentice.

In a month's time, he was sufficiently recovered from his wounds and the fevers that came with them, and was well enough to return to Smith's Garrison to request leave from General Winslow, for he desired to return home. But the general pleaded and persuaded him to remain with the army, even though Benjamin still had tents in his wounds and was so lame he required two men to help him mount his horse.

At the end of January, as more of the wounded returned, Winslow was at last able to continue the fight with an army that was now down to some nine hundred men. He intended to pursue the Narragansetts, who had fled to the north, over the border with Massachusetts and into Nipmuc territory. Benjamin came with him.

As evening fell on the first day's march, they came upon the Narragansett village of Pumham, a sachem who was known to be in support of Philip. Directly ahead, lying between them and the wigwams was an icy swamp, which prevented them from running as they had intended. As they marched forward carefully on the ice, they soon realized it was hollow in many places: a number of soldiers broke through, causing loud cracking sounds that shattered the silence and ruined any chance of surprise.

The natives were quick to answer the alarm, rising from their huts and firing upon the approaching army. Both sides were soon engaged in shooting at each other, though without result, since they were yet too far apart for their muskets to be of any effect.

As the firing continued, now seeing the considerable size of the English force, and that they were unrelenting in their assault, the natives turned and fled.

Rushing after the enemy, one of the friendly Indians, a Mohegan, pursued and seized one of the Narragansetts who had been slowed by a leg wound. He drove his captive back to the village now under the control of the English. The Mohegan brought the captive before Winslow, so that he could be examined.

Winslow called several of his officers to gather with him around the campfire to assist him with the questioning.

The captive, a young man, tall and strong, was quick to talk in his native tongue, which the Mohegan translated. "I am not a part of any army. I fired upon you English to defend my people—to join in the fight with my brothers to resist an unprovoked attack."

Benjamin studied the captive's eyes, listening carefully to the translation, for he could not understand his words. But he could see the sincerity in the manner by which he spoke. He immediately concluded the native was telling the truth and determined that there would be no value in continuing with the questioning. He looked toward Winslow and made ready to state his assessment.

But before he could speak, Mosley turned to the general. "He's a liar, sir." He turned toward the captive and continued, "Perhaps a little torture could bring out the truth."

Benjamin, still feeling lame, grabbed hold of Winslow's arm. "Sir. This man is barely an adult—his size notwithstanding. He wouldn't know a thing." He strained in the flickering light to engage the general's eyes. "There is no use to question him further."

Winslow looked at the prisoner, then one at a time at his other captains. At last he turned to Benjamin. "All right then. Put him under guard and we shall take him with us in the morning."

Mosley jumped in. "Sir. With that wound in his leg, he is only going to slow us down." He turned toward the flames, then looked straight at Winslow. "We cannot waste time with him. We should just give him a knock on the head."

Winslow stared at Mosley, then at his other captains. They nodded toward the general and muttered their agreement.

Benjamin could not believe what he was hearing. He panned around the faces lit up by the fire; some of them smiled with eagerness. He suddenly felt sick to his stomach. He saw his was the only voice for saving the young native's life. He shook himself. *This is madness*. He leaned toward Winslow, searching for the words he might speak to convince his commander of the need for grace.

But Winslow stared at the ground, avoiding eye contact with anyone, already swayed by the sentiment of the many, men who had recently suffered so harshly at the hands of the Indians. Without looking up, he nodded his consent to the execution. He turned and walked away.

The captains moved swiftly into action. They grabbed the native, intent on making sport of him as they prepared him for execution.

Benjamin bristled, seeing his countrymen act like a cat playing with a mouse before eating it. One of the captains called out to the Mohegan who had caught the prisoner, "Hey there! You caught him. You can finish him off."

The Mohegan stepped forward, smiling to be included.

Benjamin would have nothing to do with the execution. He turned to one of the captains and muttered his intention to go and tend to his horse. He hobbled away from the fire and stood among the horses. From the distance he looked back at the scene, silently sickened by the spectacle.

The men stripped the prisoner naked and wrestled to restrain him for the execution. The prisoner struggled with all his might, but at length was unable to overcome their combined strength as they pulled his arms straight out to each side. Then recognizing their intentions, and feeling the hopelessness of his situation, he yielded to it. He settled, lifted his eyes and studied the face of his executioner, resolutely awaiting his next move.

The Mohegan stepped away five paces, turned and faced the condemned. He gripped and re-gripped his hatchet in his right hand, flexing and loosening his muscles. When he was ready, he raised his hand high above his head, leaned forward with in one motion and flung his hatchet hard, directly at the captive's face.

But the prisoner was quick. He dodged his head to the side and the hatchet sailed past. And while the men holding him flinched for the impact, he jerked his arms, broke free, and ran. He darted past the Mohegan, his leg-wound notwithstanding, and sprinted in the direction of Benjamin.

No time to think, Benjamin instinctively threw his arms open and grabbed the prisoner about the chest. They scuffled a second, but the native was very strong; he slipped from his grasp, ran past the horses, and made straight for the swamp.

Now feeling like he could no longer avoid being involved, and unwilling to condone the escape, Benjamin followed, one lame man chasing after another, racing out onto the ice and into the darkness.

The Indian slipped, stumbled, and fell, then re-gathered his feet. Benjamin closed, leaped and grabbed onto him. Again they tussled, but with no clothing to take hold of, the native slipped away. He set off running for a third time, with Benjamin hot on his heels, reaching forward and flailing at the air, trying to grab at his long hair, which was all there was to hold onto.

Benjamin pushed his body, hobbled by pain in every stride, traveling farther and farther out into total darkness. He knew that if he gave up, the prisoner would surely escape. As he labored onward, the echoes of their feet on the hollow ice were so loud, he was sure that some of his English friends would hear the noise and come to his rescue; yet no one seemed to be coming. He drove himself past the pain, farther in pursuit, now wondering if the hand of God wasn't using the escape to bring a just ending to the unjust execution. *Maybe I should just let him go?*

Ahead, the Indian crashed unseeing into a large tree that lay fallen across the swamp, breast high; he cried out loud. Benjamin reached forward and grabbed him.

The Indian seized Benjamin by his hair, spun him around with power, and started twisting his neck, intending to break it. Benjamin reached back with both hands and took hold of the Indian's hair, pulling and twisting in return, butting the back of his head hard into the Indian's face, over and over, fighting with the full of his strength.

In the heat of this scuffle Benjamin heard the ice breaking from someone coming hard, lured in their direction by their grunting and groaning; it was help for one of them, but for whom he did not know.

Calling out, "*Mister Church!*" the Mohegan ran right into them, feeling at them in the dark, trying to figure out who was who. Then finding Benjamin's hands fastened in the prisoner's hair, he divided them with several swift blows of his hatchet; and with one last hack, he ended the strife.

The Mohegan tossed his arms around Benjamin and gave him a fervent hug. "Mister Church, sir, thank you, thank you for catching my prisoner. Thank you!"

Benjamin said nothing, yet gasping for air, feeling first his own neck, then reaching down to touch his aching hip. He was completely spent, but realized he was unhurt. He gasped, "And thank you. You saved my life."

Saying nothing more, the Mohegan cut off the head of the prisoner and carried it with him back to the camp where he showed it proudly to the rest of the friendly Indians. Then he gave them all an account of how "Mister Church seized the prisoner."

They all joined him in a mighty shout.

Meanwhile, Benjamin stood as a silent witness to the festivity; he mulled the horror of it, all the while playing through a range of emotions. The war had become a brutish conflict, one that had already taken the lives of a number of his friends and neighbors, and one that could have taken his own life several times. Seeing the natives prancing around the flames, carrying the severed head with such glee, he wondered if there was yet a place in the world for grace and civility.

22

THE WINTER OF 1676

Winslow's army continued in their march to the north, engaging with and killing a number of the enemy. But on February 5th, after just one week in the field, they had exhausted their supplies and were forced to return to Boston. From there, much of the army, all of them unpaid volunteers, returned to their homes to tend to farm and family. Benjamin went to Duxbury.

In the coming weeks, one bit of bad news after another filtered through the colonies. On February 10th, Lancaster was attacked by a force of four hundred Indians—a composite force of Narragansett, Nipmuc, and Wampanoag—killing fourteen settlers and taking twenty-three more captive. Eleven days later, Medfield was burned. On February 25th, Weymouth had several buildings burned, which sent all the coastal towns into panic.

As this news came to Plymouth, the council of war was called. On February 29th, Benjamin arrived at the meeting, summoned as one "well qualified and adapted to the affairs of war."

With General Winslow presiding, and on hearing several hours of opinion from the militia captains and other prominent citizens, the council concluded that an army of sixty or seventy men should be raised to protect Rehoboth and its surroundings west of Plymouth, with the recommendation that Benjamin be placed in command.

Benjamin, aware that so much expectation and responsibility was likely to be falling in his direction, sat silent as he listened to all of their deliberations. At last Winslow looked directly at Benjamin. "Now there, Mister Church, we have not heard anything from you. Do you have any concerns with this plan?"

Benjamin removed his hat and rose slowly to his feet. Out of his respect for all of those present, many of them friends, he spoke softly. "If the enemy were to return to that part of the colony, they will surely come in great numbers. And if I should take this command, I would not lie waiting for them in any town or garrison, waiting to be slaughtered on their terms; rather I should wait for them in the woods just as they would." Seeing those words penetrate the minds of the other leaders seated at the dais, particularly General Winslow, he continued, "And I would not send out such a small company against the multitudes of the enemy, which are now mustered together; for doing so would be to deliver ourselves into their hands to be destroyed." He paused, seeing them squirming in their seats, for what he had just said was hard for them to hear.

Benjamin pressed on. "I should need a force of no less than three-hundred soldiers; and the other colonies should send out their quotas as well.

He straightened tall and strengthened his voice. "Gentlemen, if we intend to make an end to this terrible war, we shall need to do so by subduing the enemy with overwhelming force. We must make a business of war, just as the enemy has."

He lowered his voice again. "I tell you, though it brings me no joy in saying this, that for my own part, I have wholly laid aside my own private business and concerns for this war, ever since the war broke out.

"But let me focus on the plan. If you should send forth such a force under my command, I would go out with them on a six-week march, which is long enough to be kept in the woods; for after that, the men will need their liberty to return. I believe that under these plans, men will go out cheerfully. Just engage one-hundred-fifty of the best soldiers, volunteers, add fifty more from the other colonies, and then one hundred friendly Indians. For with such an army, I shall gladly serve. But on any lesser terms, I must respectfully decline your commission."

Winslow studied the faces of the other leaders around him; several were visibly shaken by the request. He addressed Benjamin, "I am sure you recognize that we are already in debt from this war; and to bring together an army as you suggest would bring such charges we would never be able to pay. And I must also say, for the sake of the others here, that we consider it most inadvisable to send out Indians in our defense." He saw concurrence in the nodding heads of the other leaders, then turned to Benjamin. "No, Mister Church, I am sorry, for such a request as you propose is simply impractical."

Benjamin thought about how he might snap back at them, that *war is neither inexpensive nor is it practical.* But he was not the sort to insult people by pointing out their ignorance; his mother's upbringing would not allow him to be so rude. So he stayed silent and nodded his understanding as to their decision. He his hat back on, turned, and left.

Having seen the politicians' refusal to engage in the means necessary to resolve the war, and fearful of the consequences, Benjamin decided to move his family away from Plymouth to Aquidneck Island, which he fashioned to be a safer place for his wife and young son. He discussed his plans with family and friends, and shortly thereafter learned that word of his intended departure had made it to the war council. This created quite a stir. Hearing this news, and not a little concerned about it, Benjamin traveled to the governor's home, intending to meet with him in private.

Winslow greeted him at the door. "I have been expecting you."

The men shook hands and Benjamin stepped inside. He followed the governor directly to the parlor where the conversation began in earnest.

Winslow was strident. "Let me be direct, Benjamin. I recognize I have no power to keep you here, for I know your views as to how we should be prosecuting the war, and understand your disappointment in ours—but this departure of yours is creating no small problem for me—considering the repercussions among the populace that a prominent leader of my army acts as if Plymouth is no safe place to live."

Benjamin shook his head. "You yourself know how until now I have put this colony before my own family. But now, this decision, sir, this I make first and only for my family." He leaned forward. "I have to be with Alice now. She is seven months pregnant. My first obligation is to her and to my son, Thomas. I would take them with me to Rhode Island where they can be secure."

Winslow measured him. He knew that Benjamin's dedication to the safety and security of the colony was second to no one. He could see he was going to lose this argument. He lowered his head and sighed.

Measuring Winslow's displeasure, Benjamin had no desire to disappoint his commander. He softened his tone. "And while I am in Rhode Island, should the need arise, I will be able to serve the colony just as well from its other side."

Winslow straightened and managed a smile, for he now had a good explanation he could use to calm the council, a council scrambling to respond to a citizenry gripped by fear. He nodded. "I understand. And though I would rather you stay, you have my permission to go." He extended his hand. "I only wish I had twenty more men to send with you, men as committed as you."

Benjamin returned to Duxbury, gathered his wife and son, and traveled south to Plymouth so that he could bid farewell to her parents and to his many friends there.

Benjamin's father-in-law pleaded with him to change his course, to relocate instead to Clark's Garrison, just south of Plymouth. "It is a mighty safe place, and we will be near enough to visit as her time approaches."

But no arguments could prevail upon Benjamin. "We cannot remain any longer in these parts. We leave tomorrow."

The next morning, March 9th, they left and brought many of their friends with them. Reaching Taunton that evening, they found Captain Pierce had also just arrived with a militia party. Pierce offered to send some of his men to guard their group safely the rest of the way to Aquidneck Island. Benjamin thanked him for his respectful offer, but not wishing to delay Pierce's own plans, he refused to accept it.

Two days later, Benjamin and his small group crossed over to the island and arrived safe at Captain John Almy's house at McCorrie Point. There, they met with friends and enjoyed good entertainment.

While they were there, more bad news of the war came to them. They learned that Groton had been attacked twice, on March 2nd and March 9th. Then they heard that Clark's Garrison was attacked March 12th and eleven settlers had been killed. Benjamin felt the firm hand of Providence, grateful that he had decided not to stay there.

More reports of violence came to them. On March 13th, Groton was attacked a third time; this time the village was burned to the ground and the settlers fled to Boston. On March 25th, sixty-three militiamen and twenty natives under the command of Captain Pierce were slaughtered at Central Falls, just north and east of Aquidneck. On March 28th, a band of Narragansetts returned to their lands on the mainland, west of Providence, to gather their seed corn; while they were in the vicinity, they burned forty-five homes, dozens of barns, a sawmill, and captured much-needed English supplies. By the end of March, a dozen villages throughout New England were completely destroyed, and many more were attacked and their citizens slaughtered. Dozens more villages and towns were making plans to flee to the larger centers of Boston, Plymouth and Providence, ready to give up their farms as the planting season approached. All of New England was under siege and in a panic, with much of its population facing the previously unimaginable threat of starvation.

In the meantime, Benjamin tended to his young family amidst the comfort of his friends, waiting for the season and his opportunity to change.

23

THE SPRING OF 1676

As spring dawned in New England, word came that King Philip had spent the winter at a place called Schagticoke on the Hoosic River, north of Albany, home to the Mahicans. Philip had by then amassed an army of 2100 warriors and he was there to woo the Mahicans, and perhaps even the Mohawks, to join his cause. But New York Governor Edmund Andros, aware of Philip's presence, called upon his good relations with the Mohawks. Andros asked them to resist, well aware of the Mohawks' hatred for the Algonquin peoples. But, when Philip's men subsequently met with a small band of Mohawks in the woods and learned of their alliance with the governor, he took a different tactic to achieve his end—his men murdered the Mohawks and then spread a story that they had been slain by the English. But one of the Mohawks they had left for dead had only been wounded; and when he returned to his people, he exposed the lie for what it was. Then the Mohawks, in just retaliation, fell on Philip's army in a surprise attack, killing more than three hundred warriors, hurling many into the river. Philip and the rest of his army then fled east, back over the border and into Massachusetts. Thus, at the end of February, the war had been halted from spreading into the

165

other colonies to the west and south. Now Philip was coming back to his home, hurting, hungry, and more desperate than ever.

As April turned into May, Benjamin remained disengaged from any service in the war, now hearing the reports that continued to filter his way. He began to think of doing anything other than housework to make himself of better use, for all he'd been hearing was bad news. He no sooner had taken a tool to cut a small stick that he accidentally sliced the top of his forefinger and the one next to it half off. Smiling as he dressed the wounds, he convinced himself that he'd had no business to leave the war. He resolved to return to the army as soon as possible.

On the 12th of May, Alice gave birth to their second son, Constant. Two weeks later, sure that mother and infant were doing well, Benjamin took passage on a sloop bound for Barnstable, which landed him at Sogkonesset (Woods Hole). From there he rode to Plymouth, arriving on the first Tuesday in June. The general court happened to be in session and welcomed Benjamin. Winslow was presiding, saying, "We are glad to see you alive."

"And I am glad to see you all alive as well. I have heard on the other side of the colony the horrid destructions in Providence, Warwick, Pawtuxet, and how all over Narragansett country there are such great desolations happening as the enemy has daily prevailed against us." He told them many details of what he had heard from refugees escaping those places.

The members of the court listened intently, previously unaware of the news he was sharing, and visibly disturbed by it.

Benjamin continued. "I scarce could eat or sleep with any comfort, seeing how this conflict has disrupted everyone. For all traveling has been stopped, and no news has passed between us in such a long time. And then on my way here, seeing so many fires and so much smoke rising, I was not sure what I would find here."

The members of the court then told of the reports they had learned of violence and destruction in and around Plymouth, and beyond, from the other colonies. The last story was told by Winslow, "In late April, Captain Wadsworth, with about fifty men, left on a march to relieve Sudbury. We heard that they missed their way and fell into an ambush. Every man was slaughtered."

Benjamin listened silently.

"You were right, Benjamin. We must instead send out a larger force—" Winslow looked at the other members of the court and continued, "—and we cannot help but think it was Providence that has brought you back to us at this very moment, for we have had second thoughts regarding your plan." This was the plan that Benjamin had proposed to the war council three months beforehand.

The very next day, after much deliberation, the members of the court concluded to send out an army of two hundred men, two-thirds English and one-third Indian; and they expected that Boston and Connecticut would join with them and raise their quotas. They also asked Benjamin to return to Aquidneck to see what other forces he could muster from among those who had escaped there from Swansea, Dartmouth, and the surrounding villages.

Benjamin returned the same way he came. But when he arrived at Sogkonesset, he found that the boat he had hired and paid to take him home was not there; he had fallen victim to a sham. With no other option, he hired two friendly Indians to paddle him in their canoe, out along the Elizabeth Islands, across the mouth of Buzzards Bay, then westward along the southern New England coast, some forty miles to Aquidneck.

On the second day, as they were passing by Sakonnet point, they spied some of the local Indians upon the rocks, fishing. Benjamin urged his guides to steer in closer, so that he might speak with them. He whispered, "I have had a great mind ever since the war broke out to return here to speak with the Sakonnet."

The Indian at the front said as he pointed, "I see several are my relatives. We should not fear that they hurt us."

"I have long hoped that I could persuade them to turn away from Philip, for they never heartily loved him."

They waved toward the shore.

Those on the rocks hallooed and waved them in. But as they got closer, the Indians disappeared down in the clefts between the rocks.

Benjamin studied the empty rocks as they drew in close, not at all settled over the situation. He turned suddenly to his guides and shouted, "Pull away! They can too easily fire upon us."

Again at a safe distance, the enemy reappeared, this time calling out in their native language, "Do come ashore, for we want to speak with you."

The guides in the canoe answered. But those on the rocks were unable to hear due to the pounding of the surf.

Benjamin called out to them and used his hands; he eventually was able to communicate his intention to meet with two of them on the beach. He pointed to the spot, out in the open, well away from the places where anyone could lay in hiding and fire upon him. They headed in toward the shore.

When they landed, Benjamin and one of his guides walked up to the top of the beach. There, he deliberately laid his musket down. He stepped well away from it and waved his arms out, showing he held no weapon.

Two Sakonnets came running toward them along the top of the strand. Neither had a gun, but one was holding a lance.

As they drew close, Benjamin immediately recognized one of them as Honest George. He smiled and extended his hand. "You wanted to speak with me?"

"Yes, Mister Church. I knew it you as soon as I hear sound of your voice. I very glad to see you alive."

They shook.

"And Awashonks be glad to see you and speak with you as me." He took a deep breath and looked far out over the water. "She left Philip." He turned back and looked directly into Benjamin's eyes. "And she not ever return to him no more. She weary of war with English."

Benjamin eased, hardly believing what he was hearing. He nodded. "Where is she?"

"About three miles from here—in swamp." He pointed. "You wait here. I run and fetch her."

Benjamin shook his head. "If I wait here, I am sure some Mount Hopes or Pocassets will find me and give me a knock on the head."

"You right, Mister Church."

He placed his hand on Honest George's shoulder and smiled. "I am not worried about the Sakonnet."

The two then made plans to meet again at the lower end of Richmond's farm where there was a large rock, a well-known spot along the coast.

"I would speak with you and Awashonks, her son Peter, and Nompash—he is a good man—and no one else. I will meet you in two days; but if it is stormy, on the next fine day."

Giving each other their hands, they parted.

Benjamin went home, carrying with him a sudden sense of hope.

24

The next morning, Benjamin went south and west to Newport, where the members of the Rhode Island General Court were sequestered and in session. There, he informed them of his recent meeting with the Sakonnet Indians and his immediate plans to return there and continue the discussion. "With your permission, I would take with me Daniel Wilcox, because he understands the native language."

Having heard the sum of Benjamin's plans, several of them spoke.

"Mister Church, you must surely be *mad*."

"After all of the service you have done for us, and the many dangers you have escaped, now you would be throwing your life away."

"The rogues will surely kill you as soon as you cross over."

"You should not run the risk."

Shaking their heads, they refused to grant their official permission.

Benjamin appealed. "It has ever been in my thoughts since the war broke out, that if I could discourse with the Sakonnet Indians, I could draw them off from Philip and employ them against him. But, until now, I have not been

171

able to have the opportunity to speak with them—" he paused and studied their faces, "—and I am loath to lose it."

The discussion continued impassioned.

One conceded, "If you go, you should take only the two Indians that came with you."

But the others concluded, "We will give you no permit—nothing from us. You are on your own."

Benjamin studied their faces, understanding their resolve. But his resolve was even stronger. "Gentlemen. I am going." He put his hat on and turned to leave.

"We are sorry to see you so resolute, Mister Church; for if you go, we do not ever expect to see your face again."

Benjamin left. He returned to his family at McCorrie Point.

He arose early the next morning, the day appointed for the meeting, and prepared two light canoes for the trip. The weather was fine, the surf calm, so there would be no impediment to their trip. He had been fortunate to continue the employment of his two Indian guides and was able to convince Daniel Wilcox also to accompany him. They joined him early to help him finish loading the supplies.

Standing beside the water and feeling now ready to depart, he turned and looked up to the top of the beach. Alice stood holding the baby, with three-year-old Thomas standing at her side. He asked his men to wait for a moment and walked up to say goodbye.

Alice studied his eyes. "I do not want you to go. Really." Her face reddened. "I am not at all at peace about this."

Benjamin wrapped one arm around her and the baby; with his other he cupped the tender face of Thomas. "You have seen how God has protected me thus far, in such amazing ways. For I know that He is the one who protects me all the time, whether I stay here, or whether I go." He looked into her eyes and smiled. "I believe I must go and do this, and continue to trust Him. And He will watch you three while I am way."

Alice reached up and swept the tears from her eyes. She nodded.

He looked at her another long moment. Then thinking he could delay no longer, he kissed them each goodbye.

Benjamin returned to where the others stood waiting. Nodding to them as they took hold of their canoes, they together shoved out into the water and departed.

They crossed directly over toward the eastern side of the river, then turned south, floating on the receding tide, paddling their way several miles along the shore. Then drawing near to Richmond's farm, he could see ahead several Indians sitting upon the rock above the beach, waiting for their arrival. Keeping a safe distance away, Benjamin sent one of his native guides ashore in the second canoe, so that he might determine if these were the Indians whom he had requested to meet, and no more.

From the distance, Benjamin watched with interest as one of the natives came down to greet his guide. There, the two discoursed for a few minutes before his guide traded places with the native, who entered the canoe and paddled out toward Benjamin. As he drew close, he could see it was George waving to him. All was proceeding according to his plan.

Benjamin and Daniel went ashore with George, leaving the second guide in the other canoe to watch the event from afar. He intended him to remain in a safe position to be able to carry the news away, should the pretense of the meeting prove to be false.

As they were paddling, Benjamin called forward to George, who was at the front of the canoe, "Are Awashonks and the other Indians I asked for—are they here?"

"Yes, Mister Church."

"Are there any more Indians?"

"Awashonks here." George kept his eyes forward as he paddled hard through the surf, giving no other answer.

Benjamin stared at the back of George's head, knowing his question had not been answered. He tightened his grip on the oar as they pulled ahead and onto the beach.

No sooner had they landed and pulled the canoe above the line of the tide but Awashonks and the others Benjamin had requested rose up and came down to meet them.

Awashonks extended her hand. "Mister Church, I glad see you."

Benjamin smiled as he took hers. "How long I have waited to see you again. Too long."

One at a time both parties greeted each other with handshakes and happy expressions.

Through the translator, Awashonks expressed her gratitude that Benjamin was "willing to expose himself, to take the risk in coming to this meeting."

He nodded.

They walked together up the beach a gunshot distance from the water where there was a convenient place to sit, right where the sand ended.

At once a great body of Indians rose up from hiding in the tall grasses, grass as high as a man's waist. They stepped forward and briskly surrounded them, closing them in, armed with guns, spears, knives, and hatchets, and with their hair trimmed and faces and bodies painted for war.

Benjamin stared silently at Awashonks, his jaw set.

Her eyes fixed on his.

The natives surrounding them stood quiet and still.

Benjamin could feel his heart pounding in his chest. He took a deep breath. At last he spoke softly to her through Daniel. "George informed me that you had a desire to see me, and to discourse about making peace with the English."

She nodded. "Yes."

"Then it is customary, when people meet to negotiate for peace, to lay aside their arms, and to not appear in such a hostile form as your people do." He looked around at the warriors. "So if we are to talk about peace—as I desire to do—then your men might lay aside their arms to appear more treatable."

When Daniel finished translating, an angry murmur swept through the warriors.

Awashonks turned to them and raised her hands to calm them. She turned back to Benjamin and asked through the translator, "Which arms should they lay down, and where?" She smiled.

Studying now the very surly faces, and feeling the danger, he measured his response. "Only the guns—and at some small distance—" he pointed, "—and only for formality's sake."

The grumbling stopped as the warriors with one accord nodded and stepped away. They laid down the guns and returned.

They all sat down.

Benjamin lifted the cord of his calabash from over his head. He removed the cork, raised the vessel, and looked at her. "I trust you haven't lived so long out west with Philip that you have forgotten how to have a good strong drink." He tilted the gourd toward her, then raised it to his lips, studying her face as she watched him. He perceived she was wondering whether he would swallow any of the rum.

He offered her the gourd.

She motioned with her hand that he should have the first drink.

"There is no poison in it." He poured some of the liquid into his palm, sipped it, then lifted the gourd and took a good drink.

The natives all rose to their feet.

Benjamin looked up at them. "You will not drink for fear there should be poison in it?"

He rose up and handed the shell to a native standing beside her, who quickly raised it to his mouth and took several gulps.

Benjamin put his hand to the native's throat and seized the bottle from him. "*Do you intend to swallow this, shell and all?*"

He handed the gourd to Awashonks.

She studied Benjamin's face a moment as her lips curled into a grin. She took a good hearty drink, wiped her lips with the back of her wrist, and then passed it among her attendants.

Benjamin pulled out a roll of tobacco he had purchased the day before and distributed it as they began to talk, all through the interpreter.

Awashonks began. "Why is it, Mister Church, that you promised me a year ago you would return, and you have not come to the Sakonnet until now? For if you had come as you promised, we probably never would have joined with Philip against the English."

"When the war broke out so suddenly, I was called immediately into service. Yet afterwards, I did come down as far as Punkatees, where a great many Indians attacked us and fought against me for a whole afternoon—even though I had not come to fight them. I had with me fourteen men. My main design was to discourse with some Sakonnet Indians."

Upon hearing the words of the translator, a loud murmur arose, talking first, then shouting. Fierce and violent expressions came over the warriors. They rose with one accord, and a great surly one of them raised up his club and jerked toward Benjamin, determined to bash him in the head, screaming in his native tongue. But some of the others reached out and grabbed him, preventing the native from getting close enough.

Benjamin stood. Daniel rose up and leaned toward Benjamin's ear. "Did you understand what he said?"

"No," said Benjamin, shaking his head.

"He said that you killed his brother at Punkatees, and now he thirsts for your blood."

Benjamin turned to Daniel. "You tell him that his brother began first. And if he had kept to Sakonnet, according to my desire and instruction, then he should not have been hurt." He stared at the angry man, unflinching.

Awashonks' son, Peter, the chief commander of the group, rose to his feet. He commanded everyone to "Silence! We should talk no more about old things."

Faces reluctantly eased. Everyone sat back down.

Benjamin resumed. "Tell me the terms you would want in order to break your league with Philip. I will carry them to my masters and share them. Now you must realize that it is not in my power to conclude peace with you. But I know that if your proposals are reasonable, that the English government will not be unreasonable, and I will use all of my interest to negotiate in your behalf." He waited until the translator finished speaking, studying their expressions before he continued, "You remember how the Pequots once made war with the English, and that afterwards they subjected themselves to the English—and how the English then became their protectors against the nations that would otherwise have destroyed them."

Benjamin watched as they listened and as they nodded.

The discussion continued and many voices joined in.

At length, the Sakonnet concluded to lay aside their weapons and to submit to the Plymouth government—on the promise that their lives would be spared and that none of them would be transported out of the country.

"Then I am well satisfied that Plymouth will readily concur with this proposal." Benjamin turned to Peter and extended his hand. "I am pleased with the thought of your return to friendship, that we may resume the good relations we had before."

Peter took his hand and smiled, then tilted his head in respect. "Sir, please accept me and my men. We fight for you, and help give you Philip's head before corn is ripe. And we fight with you as long as English have one enemy left in country." The others round him rose and nodded in agreement.

Benjamin hadn't expected such an offer. He rolled the idea around in his mind, then recognized the Sakonnet could be perfect allies to fight with him—just what he needed. A smile formed on his face. "If you will do this, stay true to your word, then I and my children will be fast friends to you and to your children." He shook many of their hands, now barely containing his joy.

Benjamin realized there remained certain formalities and set down to the business of executing the treaty. "I would like you to choose five men to accompany me to Plymouth."

Wishing to be accommodating, Peter shook his head. "No, Mister Church. You choose best men to go."

Benjamin smiled deferentially, appreciating the depth of their concession. Still, he preferred to engage their involvement in the process. At length it was agreed between them that Peter and Awashonks should choose three and Benjamin would choose the other two.

"I shall return to the island tonight and will come back to you tomorrow morning. We shall go through the woods to Plymouth."

Peter wagged his head. "No. Woods not safe for you. For enemy might meet and kill you, and then we lose our friend, and our plan for peace will fail."

Benjamin acceded to their concerns and agreed they would travel over water. They chose a meeting place. "It may take me some time to obtain a vessel. I shall come as soon as I am able."

Peter, Awashonks, and all those standing with them agreed to the plan.

Then Benjamin and his men walked away, back down to the water. There they turned and looked back up the beach at all of the natives standing there. They waved happily, pushed their canoe out into the surf and pulled hard back toward Aquidneck, refreshed by a first measure of success.

25

After Benjamin returned to Aquidneck, he traveled to Newport to secure a vessel that would take him and the Sakonnets to Plymouth. Explaining his intentions to a number of mariners, he found no one willing to take him. Boats were suddenly and surprisingly "unavailable," or "not headed in that direction." These excuses were obviously lies, for he could read their faces, which were filled with fear and doubt—fear due to fresh memories of death and destruction, and doubt because they distrusted Benjamin's optimism. And as one seaman after another excused himself and walked away, Benjamin found himself questioning his own hope that there could ever again be peace between English and Indian.

After a week of failing to secure a vessel, Providence raised up a new challenge: the weather turned unseasonably stormy. The sea kicked up by such strong winds that maritime commerce came to a halt. Now he wondered if God was telling him to stop. Benjamin's heart sank. Again he had been unable to keep his promise to Awashonks.

At length, a fully loaded vessel arrived from the east and landed at the pier. Benjamin introduced himself to the owner, Mister Anthony Low.

181

Though the two had never met, Anthony was well acquainted with Benjamin's exploits in the war. "I am delighted to meet with you, for I am so pleased with all you are doing in fighting for us."

Benjamin explained his current need.

Anthony responded with a broad grin, "I will run the venture and am very glad to wait upon you."

The next morning, they set sail behind a stiff westerly that soon brought them to Sakonnet Point. But upon arriving there, the wind turned hard into their face. Suddenly the waves rose and the surf pounded their small vessel, preventing them from getting any closer to the land for fear of running aground.

Benjamin looked toward the shore and saw a handful of Indians waiting for them on the rocks. He recognized Peter Awashonks, called to him, and they waved to each other.

Seeing the violence of the sea, it was doubtful what next to do. Yet Peter made no hesitation. He climbed into a small canoe and paddled himself out to them through the waves. Coming alongside, they tossed him a line. He seized hold of it, and with great struggle, while he was bobbing up and down and side to side, he pulled himself up and into their boat. Peter scrambled to his feet, very happy to be aboard.

At that moment the rain arrived in torrents and the wind blew them sideways, up and into the sound. Looking down over the side, Peter's canoe was gone, a victim to the waves.

Seeing now no more opportunity or means to take anyone else on board, they turned north, riding with the wind up to Bristol Ferry, then round the northern end of the island where they tacked their way south, back to Newport, carrying Peter with them.

Now having heard the surprising news that the army would be arriving the next day, and seeing the present impossibility of traveling east by water, Benjamin thought of a different approach to accomplish his design. He dismissed Mister Low with a hearty handshake, grateful for his assistance, and took Peter with him directly back to Almy's house.

Benjamin spent the afternoon and evening writing an account of his transactions with the Indians and also drew up the proposals, the articles of peace, with the intent to present these to His Honor, Governor Winslow, if he might see cause to sign them. Then the next afternoon, Sunday, June 25th, seeing the army was now two days past their appointed arrival, he grew weary of waiting and made his decision. He sent Peter with the letter and articles of peace to deliver these overland to Plymouth, first stopping at Sakonnet to gather up the other Indians who had been appointed to go with him.

On Tuesday, after a long-overdue day of rest, Benjamin traveled with Alice and some friends to Portsmouth on the pretense of picking cherries, intent instead on hearing something of the army. But they returned home without any news. Then just before midnight, Benjamin was roused from his sleep with an express from Major Bradford, who had arrived with the army at Pocasset.

He left immediately and arrived at the fort as the sun was coming up, going straight into a private meeting with the major.

Bradford listened intently to the full of Benjamin's report of all his proceedings with the Sakonnet. Then he spoke. "And I have a word for you."

Benjamin leaned forward.

"Last month, Captain William Turner of the Massachusetts Brigade marched with one-hundred-fifty men to bring relief to the western towns. Learning that Philip had kenneled himself nearby in the Wetuset Hills on the banks of the Connecticut River, he ventured a midnight attack on one of the enemy camps. Turner and his men found the Indians sound asleep beside a roaring cataract, which had concealed the sound of their approach. Then entering their teepees, they killed many of the enemy as they slept, and roused the rest, who took off in a panic, screaming 'Mohawks!' for they had been confused by the darkness and the fog of sleep. Most fled through the trees and down the hillside to the river, hoping to escape. There, they jumped into their canoes, shoved of, and fumbled in the gloom for their paddles. And being so disoriented, several hundred of the Indians were caught in the current and swept over the falls where they drowned."

Bradford's face turned sullen. "But a great company of Philip's men were also encamped nearby, on the east side of the river. And having been awakened by the gunfire, they came to the native camp, where they surprised Turner and his men who had been occupied with killing the last of the natives in their teepees. The army fled under the counterattack, back to their horses, and escaped to Hatfield, all the while under the hot pursuit of one thousand of Philip's warriors. Some fifty English fell along the way, and Turner was among them."

Benjamin studied Bradford's face as he finished, a face now lined with worry, struggling to form what words to say next. But Benjamin knew what he was thinking. "Then Philip is coming back here, isn't he?"

Bradford nodded. "And this peace with Awashonks—let us just say that it could not have come at a better time."

The two formulated a plan of action, and with the Major's consent, Benjamin returned the next morning to Aquidneck, to make ready to return again to Awashonks to inform her that the army had just arrived.

That afternoon he departed alone in a small canoe from Sachuest Neck—in the southeast corner of the island—

pushing off while the tide was slack, and braving his way across the two-and-a-half miles of open water to Sakonnet, on the east side of the sound.

Benjamin walked up into the native camp and was greeted there by George, who escorted him directly into a meeting with Awashonks, serving as translator. There, he told her that Major Bradford had just arrived at Pocasset with a great army, and that he (Benjamin) had explained to the major all of her intentions and plans for peace. "He is ready to meet with you; and requests that you come."

Awashonks appeared visibly shaken, for the plan had changed.

He smiled to reassure her. "If you will simply meet with him as he has requested, then you need not have any fear of being hurt by them. You should call all of your people together. And do not permit any stragglers who could be confused as not being a party to the peace. Then after I have spoken again with the major, I shall meet with you again, here, tomorrow, and give you further word."

She measured him, then nodded. "I shall gather my people together. But you must realize it will be difficult on such short notice."

Benjamin returned again to the island, rode hard to the ferry, and crossed over to the army that same night in Pocasset.

On Thursday morning, the whole army marched south toward Sakonnet, making it as far as Punkatees where they pitched their tents. There, Bradford dispatched Benjamin with a half-dozen men to meet with Awashonks, to call her down to the English camp.

As they were going south, they met a Pocasset Indian who had killed a cow and was carrying a quarter of it on his back and its tongue in his pocket. The Indian showed no resistance and cordially introduced himself, telling them his name was Toby; then freely gave them an account of how he had come down there two days prior with his mother and several other Indians, having left a group of his people behind, and now they were hiding in the nearby swamp.

Seeing how Toby was both amicable and full of information that might be of good use, Benjamin disarmed him and sent him with two of his men back to Major Bradford for questioning.

It was late in the afternoon when Benjamin and his companions arrived at Awashonks' camp. There, he told her, "I am here to invite you and all your people to come down to Punkatees to meet with Major Bradford, for all of the Plymouth army is encamped there. There, you and all your subjects can receive your orders from the government."

Awashonks sighed with relief, relief that peace was finally coming, and visibly resigned to the next step in the process. She spoke through her translator, "Several of my people are not yet here. I will gather them in and we shall come down to the English camp tomorrow."

At noon on Friday, June 30th, Awashonks, regaled in her royal dress, and surrounded by her captains, came walking proudly out of the thickets and down onto Punkatees Neck. Following after her were most of her people, some ninety Sakonnets. Benjamin went out to welcome her as they entered the camp and introduced them to Major Bradford.

The first of Awashonks' captains shook Bradford's hand and smiled. "I fight now with you English."

Bradford stiffened, but smiled and nodded. He glanced at Benjamin with his brow raised.

One at a time the other captains lined up and shook Bradford's hand, each smiling knowingly at him. He gave them each a firm handshake.

When the introductions were complete, Bradford leaned toward Benjamin and spoke softly, "I would like to talk with you." He tilted his head toward Awashonks, showing her his respect, turned, and walked back to his tent.

Benjamin followed.

Inside the tent, Bradford wasted no time. "Mister Church, I do have orders to restore you to duty. But I cannot have any of those Indians fighting in my army." He stared at Benjamin. "What exactly did you tell them?"

Benjamin looked back at him, dumbfounded. He swallowed. "Sir, they are grateful to be free of Philip, and anxious to demonstrate their allegiance to the English. I met with them merely to offer peace and to welcome them under our protection, if they would accept it. But then they went further, speaking out of their independence, for they have no interest in being wards of our government. They wish to fight alongside us as good neighbors."

Bradford shook his head. "But I have a problem with that, the problem of trust. I have no assurance they will not turn against us, and I know there are many in the army that would feel the same way about these people, people they still refer to as 'savages.'"

Benjamin removed his hat and held it to his chest. "William, you know that I will gratefully serve again, and would accept your commission. But I would ask respectfully that you accept the Sakonnet to fight with me against the enemy."

Bradford stepped behind his desk and sat down. He stared a moment at his papers lying there, found the one he was looking for, then looked up. "I have my orders. I can improve you, if I wish. But I—I cannot improve the Indians. I simply cannot be concerned with them. I have a war to fight with the enemy and would rather not waste any energy fighting also with my own men."

Benjamin sighed, closed his eyes, and nodded. "Yes, sir."

"Very well then. Now you tell Awashonks and all her subjects, the men, women, and children, tell them that they are to repair to Plymouth. Jack Havens will accompany them for their safety. But as to their final disposition, I leave that matter to the governor." He paused, thoughtfully. "Benjamin, when you are there, they *and you*, can make whatever appeal you wish to make directly to the governor." He extended his hand.

Benjamin took it and gave it a firm squeeze. He said, "Thank you," and stepped out of the tent.

Returning back to Awashonks, her captains approached and listened in as he gave her the major's orders. He added, "I shall meet you first in Sandwich, in six days. Then we shall go on together to meet with the governor." He stepped away and watched as the natives conversed among themselves.

After a few moments the captains approached and gathered around him. One of them spoke. "I know not why they no trust us, nor invite us to fight Philip."

Benjamin looked around at their sad faces, as his own eyes grew heavy. He nodded his understanding, then placed his hand on the shoulder of the one that spoke. "It is best that you obey the major's orders." He smiled to reassure him and the others. "It will not be more than a week and then I shall come and join with you. Then we can appeal to the governor together. For I am confident he will accept you and offer you a commission."

Then introducing them to Jack Havens, an Indian known and trusted by the English, he sent Awashonks, her captains, and all her people off toward Sandwich, with Havens at the front, carrying the white flag of truce.

26

JULY 1676

After Awashonks departed, Benjamin took Toby and several soldiers with him into the swamp and there took Toby's mother and the others that were with her as prisoners. The next morning, July 1ˢᵗ, the whole army marched north back to Pocasset. Along the way, Toby revealed that there were many of Philip's Indians who had come down to Keekamuit to eat clams there, as their provisions had become scarce.

Benjamin asked, "Which Indians are these?"

"Some Weetamoo's Indians, some Mount Hope Indians, some Narragansett Indians, and some upland Indians. In all, about three hundred." He paused and fixed his eyes on Benjamin. "And Philip himself is expected to join them in three or four days."

This news was quickly shared with Major Bradford.

When they arrived at Pocasset, a flotilla of Rhode Island boats was there to meet them, having been arranged under orders from Major Bradford. The entire army boarded, horses and all; they departed at dusk. Straight ahead they could plainly see the enemy's fires across the water, just where Toby had told them. They held their course in that direction.

But when they came to the north of Aquidneck, the lead boat, carrying Major Bradford, veered to the west. As the other boats came past Sandy Point, they did the same.

Benjamin stepped to the back of the boat to the steersman. "Where are we headed?"

The sailor looked up. "Mount Hope."

Benjamin turned and looked north, across the water at the enemy fires, feeling that yet again an opportunity to engage them directly was slipping away. Frustrated, he turned back to the steersman. "Why?"

"Just following orders."

Benjamin peered ahead at the lead boat and whispered to himself, "*He is going after Philip.*"

Landing at Mount Hope, they made straight for the enemy village, but found the place dark and empty, with no sign of Philip or anyone else having been there in a while.

Bradford's army set up camp around the perimeter, hiding in the trees as best they could, and under strict order to light no fires. They would wait for Philip to come.

By the middle of the fourth day, seeing no sign of Philip, it was clear there was no more value in waiting. They broke camp and set off for Rehoboth, to regroup and re-supply there. Along the way they stopped at Keekamuit, finding that place abandoned, the fires cold, the enemy long gone. Benjamin quietly stewed, sure that yet another opportunity of doing spoil upon the enemy had been lost.

Arriving at Rehoboth on July 6th, and seeing no more point in remaining with the army, Benjamin obtained permission from Major Bradford to go and meet with the Sakonnet, who surely by then must have reached Sandwich. Bradford offered to send several men to guard him, but he chose one man only, Samuel Sabin, to be his pilot, a man well acquainted with the woods and all the trails in that part of the territory.

At sunset, they mounted their horses, rode all night, and arrived safe in Plymouth the next morning, about two hours after sunrise. By the time they had refreshed themselves at the local inn, the governor had come to town, along with Benjamin's father-in-law.

Benjamin gave them both a short account of all that had taken place with the army, anxious to get to his point.

Winslow thanked him for his good and great service at Sakonnet. "The Indians arrived here—"

"Peter?"

"Yes. Peter. He arrived with your letter. I read all that you promised to Awashonks, your articles for peace." Winslow paused. "There were several among the council who wanted to hold Peter and his men as hostages, to guarantee the peace. But I and Constant, here, we believed it best to allow them to return unhindered, to not permit this process to unravel." He smiled at Benjamin. "I prevailed upon the council. I signed the articles of peace and we let them go."

Benjamin eased and allowed himself to smile. "Have you heard anything more from Awashonks?"

"No."

"Last Wednesday at Punkatees, Major Bradford met with her..." Benjamin explained the details of the discussion with Bradford and his decisions. "He sent her and some ninety of her subjects to Sandwich under a flag of truce. I promised to meet them, and I encouraged them that I might be able to obtain a commission from your honor to lead them forth to fight Philip."

Winslow leaned back and shook his head, trying to smile. "You should not want such a commission; neither are there enough good Englishmen to join you in your army."

Benjamin glanced at his father-in-law, then took a deep breath and faced the governor. "You honor, the time has expired for me to meet the Sakonnets at Sandwich. I should have been there yesterday."

Winslow studied Benjamin's demeanor. He acceded. "When would you go?"

"This afternoon, with your consent."

"Then how many men would you like to have with you?"

"Not more than a half-dozen, but with an order to take more at Sandwich, if I should need them. And I will need horses."

Winslow agreed and quickly wrote up the order.

Benjamin set out right away to draw out his men. Joining him were his brother-in-law, Nathaniel Southworth, and Jabez Howland, the constable of Middleborough. Benjamin looked Howland in the eye as he shook his hand, unsure of his help, wondering how he would react to working closely with natives, since his testimony had led to the conviction of the three Indians that killed John Sassamon. But he figured he would somehow measure him later to see if he could be trusted—and if not, he could be dismissed. They left right away for Sandwich and arrived that night, where Benjamin was at last able to get a few hours of sleep.

Early the next morning, Saturday the 8th, having added more men, now with sixteen, they proceeded as far as Agawom, where they had a great expectation of meeting the Sakonnet. They searched for miles and miles everywhere in the woods, along the riverbanks and around the coves and inlets, but did not find anyone. A number of his men became discouraged; ten returned. But the other half-dozen stuck by Benjamin, promising to remain with him until they found the Indians.

In the afternoon, after scouring an area of some thirty square miles, they crossed the Sippican River, heading south. Climbing up the far bank, Benjamin heard Howland sigh from exhaustion, obviously, unused to his pace. When asked, he admitted he was tired.

Benjamin pulled back on the reins and stopped. He looked around at the scenery, then at Howland. "You should wait here and rest. I am going to continue and look to the south. If we meet any of the enemy and are forced back, you will be our reserve, to help us back over the river." He left two men with him and continued.

Farther south, they crossed a small river and looked ahead to where it drained into a cove, with the wide Buzzard's Bay opening up beyond. There, they could see many miles along the shore, where there were sands and flats. As they drew closer, they could hear a great noise below them. They dismounted their horses, left them, and crept up onto the dunes. Reaching the top, they laid down in the tall grasses and peered over the edge, observing the scene.

Below, they saw a vast company of Indians of all ages: men, women, and children. Some were on horseback running races; some were kicking a ball around on the beach; others were clamming, or in the water catching eels and flatfish.

Benjamin wondered how he might safely find out which Indians they were. At length, he and his men moved farther down into a thicket. There, Benjamin called out to a group of young natives who rode near them on horseback.

Two of the natives looked up and rode straight to where they were hiding. Then on seeing they were Englishmen, and so close and armed, they spun around and rode off in a hurry.

Benjamin leaped to his feet and shouted, "*My name is Church!*"

One glanced back as he rode.

"We will not hurt you!"

They both pulled back and stopped.

"I just want to speak with you." Benjamin lay his gun down and raised both hands, showing them empty.

The young men turned their horses and returned halfway, interested, but wary.

"Who are these Indians?" Benjamin asked.

One of the boys, a teenager, spoke. "We are Sakonnet. Awashonks is here."

"Is Jack Havens here?"

"Yes." He turned and pointed at him.

"Would you go and get him? I should like to speak with him. And do tell Awashonks also I am here to meet with her."

The young man smiled, showing his own relief. Immediately the two turned and rode straight down the beach toward Jack Havens.

Benjamin and his men stood now in the open and watched from a distance as his message was delivered, then seeing the natives' reactions as they turned and pointed back in their direction.

Jack Havens came and happily extended his hand. They exchanged a few words. He added, "Awashonks and all her company have treated me kindly."

By this time, a whole company of Indians came riding up to them on horseback, well-armed, but wearing pleasant expressions, waving and greeting Benjamin and his men with respect.

Benjamin removed his hat, smiled broadly at each of them. He tilted his head forward in deference to their kind greetings; the three English who with him did the same. He turned again to Havens, "Would you kindly go and tell Awashonks? Tell her that I would like to sup with her this evening—and I should like to lodge here in her camp this night."

Havens nodded and walked away.

Taking some of the Indians with him, Benjamin went back to the river to look for Mister Howland and the others. And having an idea he should now put Howland to a test to see what sort of soldier he might be, he concocted a plan. He grinned as he shared it with the Indians and told them how they should each act out their parts.

When they neared the place, Benjamin and his three English companions rode hard out ahead of the natives, pretending to be fleeing an attack. Then they turned and fired into the sky above the Indians as they followed, who likewise were firing errant shots back above their heads.

Howland, being on guard, hearing the guns, and seeing the action, concluded his friends were in distress. He leaped onto his horse and rode hard to join Benjamin, raising his musket, taking aim, and ready to fire at the Indians.

Looking down the open muzzle of Howland's musket, Benjamin suddenly realized the game he had devised had the potential for disaster. He pulled back hard on his reins and thrust his hand up high, signaling everyone to halt. His horse skidded to a stop, as did the horses of the Indians that were following behind him. He stared ahead at Howland with his heart pounding, hoping he too would stop.

Howland flinched. He glanced at the Indians behind Benjamin, seeing that the "enemy" had also responded to his captain's command. He slowed and came to a halt, for he now understood "the game," and that he had become their source of entertainment. He lowered his gun, relaxed, and smirked out a grin.

Benjamin breathed a sigh of relief as everyone with him burst into laughter.

Howland rode slowly the rest of the way up to Benjamin, who was by now surrounded by the Sakonnets, each of them wearing broad smiles. Howland studied them, then Benjamin. He monotoned, "I suppose you found the Indians."

"I suppose we did."

And after Benjamin and his companions slapped the good-natured Howland on the back and told him the full of their news, they gathered the rest of Howland's men and hastened back down to Awashonks' camp.

Upon their arrival, Benjamin and his men were conducted to a small shelter where Awashonks and her captains came and greeted them. The natives were glad to see Benjamin, and the fulfillment of his promise—so glad that the whole multitude of them shouted. The woods rang with their joy.

At sunset, all the natives came running from their quarters, each loaded with the tops of dry pines. They made a huge pile of them in front of the open side of the shelter. Then they brought supper in three dishes: bass in one dish, eels and flatfish in the second, and shellfish in the third.

When they finished eating, they made ready to set the fire. All of the Indians, young and old, great and small, gathered in three rings around the pile of branches. Awashonks, with the oldest of her people, men and women, knelt down and formed a first ring, closest to the fire; then all the men, the strong and stout, made a second ring; and all the rest surrounded the outside. The small flame was placed in among the branches. It spread quickly until the whole of the pile of dry needles and pine knots erupted in a massive explosion of heat and light.

Then Peter Awashonks stepped between the rings and the fire. He carried a spear in one hand, a hatchet in the other, and began to dance around the fire, thrusting his spear in at the flames, fighting with them, and calling out the names of all the Indian nations that were at war with the English.

"Narr-a-gan-setts!"

And at the naming of each of the tribes, he thrust his spear in and drew out a firebrand and fought with it using the end of his spear.

"Nip-mucs!"

And at the finishing of the fight with each firebrand, as it grew cold and dim, he bowed down to it and thanked it.

"Nash-a-way!

"Po-dunks!

"Po-cass-ets!

"Pok-a-nok-ets!

"Wamp-a-no-ags!"

When he had finished naming and fighting all of the nations, he thrust his spear and hatchet down into the sand and stepped out of the ring. Then another of his captains rose up and did the same dance, with more fury, if possible, than his predecessor.

When a half-dozen of the chiefs had acted out their parts, Peter approached Benjamin, who was seated in the shelter, resting his hands on his knees, fully engrossed in the dance. Peter leaned close and told him, "We making soldiers for you, making ready, and swearing to fight for English."

Benjamin smiled up at him. He nodded.

Completing the dance, having engaged all the strong and stout men, Awashonks stood and came close to Benjamin, surrounded by her dancers.

Benjamin and his Englishmen stood.

She spoke. "Mister Church. You call any these men to fight for English. Call any you want, or all, anytime you need. They *fight* for you." One of her subjects handed her a flintlock, which she presented to Benjamin.

He glanced down at the weapon and took it in both hands, examining it. It was a showpiece, fine and polished.

He looked directly at her and smiled, tilting his head forward in respect.

Before sunrise the next morning, having drawn out two-dozen of the Sakonnet, including Peter, they set out for Plymouth and arrived there that same day.

Having been informed of the news of their arrival, Governor Winslow came to town the next morning, Monday, July 10th. It was there, before friends and family, that he commissioned Benjamin, and gave to him two-dozen English volunteers to join with his Indians who were all now under his command, that they might go out together in quest of the enemy.

Part Three

27

Having marched all night through the woods, Benjamin and his half-Indian-half-English company arrived in Middleborough before the sun came up. And as soon as the light appeared, they set off into the swampy thickets, following intelligence they had received as to where some Narragansett and Mount Hope Indians might be hiding. Seeing several lines of smoke curling into the sky, Benjamin paused their motion and sent one of his Sakonnets ahead as a scout. The report came back soon enough, complete with details of the enemy camp, the number present, and their degree of readiness; there were no guards posted.

Benjamin gave his orders, spreading his men out quickly to the left and right, encircling and surrounding the camp. As soon as they all were in place, they burst forward out of the thickets on every side, shouting with one accord, wielding their guns and hatchets. This so surprised the enemy that Benjamin's men had no need to fire a shot; they disarmed everyone, and not one of the enemy escaped. They took twenty captives.

Upon strict examination, one of the captives by the name of Jeffrey told Benjamin of another group of the enemy that was camped at a place called Munponset Pond. Then

201

hustling the captives back through the woods to Plymouth, they disposed of them all there with the government, except for Jeffrey, who offered to guide Benjamin to the enemy hiding places. Benjamin studied the captive and made a decision. "If you will remain faithful to me, I will make sure you are not sold out of the country." He extended his hand to the native.

Jeffrey looked Benjamin in the eye, took his hand, smiled, and shook it.

While they were in Plymouth, Benjamin met with the war council to discuss the matter of compensation, for each of his men was serving on a voluntary basis and subsisting on his own provisions. The council ruled that the government would provide the army with ammunition and provisions, but would keep half of the captives and arms that his army might bring in; they would allow the bounty for the other half to be divided among Benjamin and his English soldiers; and the Indian soldiers were permitted to keep all of the loose plunder. Benjamin argued against these arrangements. He believed strongly that his men should be better paid—considering they were risking their lives, while the council politicians had virtually nothing to lose; but mostly he detested the practice of taking bounty. Yet his arguments came to no effect. But being faced with the crueler thought of disbanding his army and allowing someone else to go out after and kill every Indian he saw, he acceded to the compensation, intending to exercise whatever personal privilege he could to show mercy and save some of the captives from being sold out of the country.

After a brief rest and resupply, they went back out again to Munponset Pond. There, they captured a dozen Narragansetts who were found fishing. They brought these all in, with none of them escaping.

They continued this stratagem for several weeks, never returning to Plymouth empty handed. When they lacked intelligence as to where the enemy was next encamped, they would spread out along the trails and lay low in hiding, waiting until an Indian traveler would happen along. In this way, they never had to wait more than a day or two until they would surprise and fall on someone unsuspecting, seeking always to capture the enemy unhurt rather than to injure or kill. Then under Benjamin's questioning, the captives would yield up the enemy positions, or even agree to guide them there in exchange for freedom and service in his company. And by this method of secret and sudden surprises, they took in great numbers of prisoners, while not one of Benjamin's men suffered injury.

And when he took prisoners, he would examine them and pick out some and tell them that if they would agree to fight with him, to become one of his soldiers, then they would be free to serve and not be sold out of the country. If he perceived that they were surly and angry, and even if Peter and his Sakonnets called them "treacherous dogs," then he would appeal to them, "Do not be so wild and surly. Because some of these, my best soldiers here, were the same way a little while ago. If you will come and fight with me for one day, you will see what I am like, and that I can be trusted." And his judgment proved always to be true, for when the captives saw how cheerful and successful all of his men were, and how they cared and watched out for one another, they became convinced. His men were becoming like brothers and his army was increasing in number.

When the government observed Benjamin's courage and conduct, and the success he was achieving, which Benjamin always credited to heaven, Winslow issued this order to enlarge his commission:

Capt. BENJAMIN CHURCH, you are hereby nominated, ordered, commissioned, and empowered to raise a company of volunteers of about two hundred men, English and Indians (the English not exceeding the number of sixty) of which company or so many of them as you can obtain, or shall see cause at present to improve, you are to take the command and conduct, and to lead them forth now and hereafter, at such time and unto such places within this colony or elsewhere within the Confederated Colonies as you shall think fit: to discover, pursue, fight, surprise, destroy, or subdue our Indian enemies, or any part or parties of them that by the providence of God you may meet with, or them, or any of them, by treaty and composition to receive mercy, if you see reason, provided they be not murderous rogues or such as have been principal actors in those villainies. And forasmuch as your company may be uncertain, and the persons often changed, you are also hereby empowered, with the advice of your company, to choose and commission a lieutenant, and to establish sergeants and corporals as you see cause. And you, herein improving your best judgment and discretion and utmost ability, are faithfully to serve the interest of God, his Majesty's interest, and the interest of the Colony, and will carefully govern your said company at home and abroad. These shall be unto you full and ample commission, warrant and discharge. Given under the public seal, this 24th day of July, 1676.

Per JOS. WINSLOW, Governor.

28

Major Bradford had moved his army to Taunton. Being short of supply, and having learned that Benjamin was yet in Plymouth, he sent orders for the captain to accompany and guard the delivery of a line of carts laden with goods to feed and equip his men.

Benjamin took the order and raised an additional dozen English volunteers to guard the supplies as far as Middleborough, so that he and his company could ride out in front of them in search of the enemy, to secure the safe delivery of the provisions. They left in the early evening, intending to travel under the protection of darkness, having agreed to meet again the next morning in Nemasket.

Benjamin and a dozen of his Indians arrived at the place of meeting just as the stars faded in the eastern sky; the sun would soon be rising. Immediately, they discovered a company of the enemy, asleep in their camp. Seeing the element of surprise as better than waiting for the rest of his troop, they charged directly into the camp, startled, and captured all of them—sixteen Indians—then placed them under guard. One at a time, Benjamin pulled them aside for questioning.

Under examination, one of the older men revealed, "Tispaquin is at Assawompset, with a great company."

Benjamin snapped into focus. Tispaquin, a near relation of Philip, was one of chief proponents of the violence and destruction in the English villages in that part of the colony; Assawompset was just seven miles distant. His immediate thought was to rush there and to engage the enemy directly, while the information was fresh. But remembering his orders were first to deliver the carts, he relented; this opportunity would have to wait. And thinking on it further, he saw the potential for disaster should the food and munitions fall into enemy hands, resupplying Tispaquin's army. Still, this knowledge gave him an idea.

When the rest of his company finally arrived, he ordered them to guard the prisoners and to wait there for the arrival of the carts. Then taking two of his men with him, he raced ahead to Taunton.

Just north of the village, he came upon a small company of English soldiers stationed on the banks at the bend of the river. He hailed a young sergeant and rode up close to speak with him. "I am Captain Church. I need to speak with Major Bradford, or one of his captains."

"They are all in town; at the tavern."

Benjamin stared at the sergeant. At the same time he knew it was yet another half mile to the center of the village, and he didn't want to waste any more time. He glanced around at the other men nearby, and then turned back to the sergeant. "Who is the ranking officer here?"

"Lieutenant Lawrence." He pointed.

Benjamin dismounted, left his horse, and walked over to the lieutenant. He introduced himself. "I have a line of carts, full of supplies for Major Bradford—" he pointed, "—ten miles that way, down this road."

Lawrence removed his hat and ran his fingers through his long, sweaty hair. The morning was very humid, and he seemed in no hurry. "I am sure Major Bradford will be glad to hear they are coming." He turned and pointed in the other direction, toward the town center. "You know he is in the village. He would be glad to see you there."

Benjamin wrinkled his lips and wagged his chin side to side. "I need to dispose of these carts."

The lieutenant placed his hand on the large rock at his side and leaned against it. His face went blank.

Anxious to return in pursuit of Tispaquin, Benjamin recognized he didn't need to explain himself to the lieutenant. He had all the authority he needed from the governor. "*Lieutenant.*"

Lawrence looked up at him.

"I am under orders to pursue and *destroy* the enemy, and I cannot be encumbered any longer with the delivery of *carts*. I am ordering you and two dozen of your horsemen to saddle up and return with me; to take over the guard of the supplies, and to bring them back here to the Major; so that I can be at liberty." He pulled out his papers and showed them to Lawrence.

Lawrence stood, leaned forward and glanced at them, noting the governor's seal and signature. He straightened. "Yes, sir."

"Send one of your men into the village to let the Major know of my instructions."

At length, the lieutenant gathered his men. They saddled up and rode with haste behind Benjamin back to Nemasket.

Finding the carts had arrived safely there, Benjamin ordered Lawrence to divide his men: "Post some with the prisoners and with the rest take the carts to Taunton; then return the carts, along with the prisoners, to Plymouth. But you are to return by Bridgewater." Benjamin judged it best to change his movements, to avoid setting a pattern visible to the enemy.

Free now to resume his pursuit, and seeing the afternoon was waning, he proposed that they press south some seven miles to encamp that night at Assawompset neck. But as they came to the swamp and the brook that runs from the north end of Long Pond into the great Assawompset Pond, a group of the enemy suddenly rose up from the tall grasses and fired upon them; then they turned and ran; but not a man of Benjamin's was hurt. Benjamin's Indians did not hesitate to respond. They rode right after the enemy into the swamp, returning fire. But because it was already dusk, the enemy escaped unseen into the thickets.

As darkness engulfed them, Benjamin and his company continued their movement a mile into the neck. It was a clear evening, but there was no moon. They had only the light of the stars to guide their way. They proceeded in a slow and steady march.

They came upon a small clearing where there was good grass, so they took advantage to stop and feed their horses. Benjamin stationed two-dozen men to stand by and hold the horses by their bridles as they fed, to keep them quiet. He spread the rest out around their perimeter to listen for the enemy. As they stood quietly by, they could hear the sounds of enemy voices in the woods on every side surrounding them; some were very near. Everyone stayed on high alert.

After several hours watch, no longer hearing the enemy, who had either left or were still for the night, Benjamin ordered his men to march quietly out of the neck. This time they went the other way, south toward the abandoned English village of Acushnet. Benjamin feared they would have been ambushed had they departed by the way they came in.

They passed through Acushnet as the waning moon came up, shining its light on the black rubble of the houses and barns. The stone chimneys were all that remained standing; the entire village had been burnt the previous summer. No one had returned to rebuild.

Continuing south, they crossed over the Acushnet River to its western bank and looked for a place to rest, having spent two nights and one day's ramble without any sleep. Finding a small clearing and good forage for the horses, Benjamin concluded they should all stop there for a nap, just for a few hours. He posted six men back at the river, guarding their path in. He ordered two men at a time to watch, taking turns, while everyone else retired to the thickets to sleep. A hush fell over their camp as they lay down.

Benjamin snapped awake to the sound of crickets. Not knowing how long he had been asleep, he looked up. It was yet night; the moon was well above the trees. He figured he had slept about four hours, a lot longer than he had intended. Rubbing the sleep out his eyes, he sat up and stretched, looking to his left and right. Those he could see were sound asleep. He leaned forward and shoved himself to his feet, feeling every inch of his body ache. He regretted he could not rest any longer, but he knew they could not remain there even another hour. They had to get going. He stepped forward out of the thickets, quietly looking for the guards, but found them lying on the ground, sound asleep beside their guns. Looking all around, his entire company had fallen victim to exhaustion. They had forgotten the danger. Not one was awake.

Quietly he roused his entire company. Then accompanied by a file of six men, he returned under the moonlight back toward the river to see what had become of his other watch.

As they stepped forward out of the tree line, their view opened up to the river. Benjamin climbed up onto a large rock and looked left, upriver, the way they had entered the neck. He saw movement.

Dropping straight down, he held his hand up for his men to stop. He rose up slowly, peering over the tops of the tall grass toward the opposite shore. A line of the enemy was moving slowly and steadily toward them, studying the ground, examining the tracks he and his men had left. He motioned quietly and quickly to his men, sending them to continue and to fetch his guard. As they skulked away, he kept his eyes fixed on the enemy as they drew closer, then stopped suddenly, stared at the water, looked all around once, and finally turned and left. He reckoned they had come to the place where he and his men had crossed the river, where their tracks had disappeared. He sighed.

In a few minutes, Benjamin's men returned crouching through the grass, having brought the six watchmen with them. Peter Awashonks crept up to Benjamin and whispered in his ear. "We found them all asleep."

Benjamin concluded they could remain there no longer.

Returning to the others, and pausing just long enough to take a little refreshment from their knapsacks, they continued an hour to the south, following along the western bank of the river until it widened out into a tidal swamp. Farther ahead the cove opened up and they rode down to the water's edge. A breeze swept in from the south, cooling them, and carrying with it the smell of the ocean. They paused a moment to study the scene. From there they could see an island at the mouth of the cove, with Buzzards Bay beyond, with its broad water shimmering in the moonlight.

There they discovered a fresh track that led away from the water and into the thickets. Benjamin ordered his men to remain with the horses, while he went ahead with Peter and a half-dozen Sakonnet to follow on foot after the track.

Soon enough they rushed in upon a small company of Indians sound asleep in their camp around a small fire. Peter recognized them right away. They were his people, Sakonnets, men, women and children.

The enemy, about a dozen, rose up to their feet and looked at Peter and Benjamin with surprise. They made no effort to run, seeing the rest of their kinsmen rushing in, brandishing their hatchets and surrounding them. Without any resistance, they surrendered themselves.

Benjamin stepped close to the leader of the group, a man he recognized. He studied the native.

The Indian glanced back at him, then looked down at the ground, obviously knowing who he was.

Peter came alongside Benjamin. "This Little Eyes. And this his family and relations."

Benjamin responded gently. "I remember him."

One of Peter's captains came up on his other side and questioned Benjamin, "You *know* him?" He leaned close. "This rogue want to *kill* you at Awashonks' dance." He clenched and shook his fist. "Now you revenge on him."

Benjamin calmly took hold of the fist. He faced his comrade and gently pressed the fist down, then spoke loud enough for all of them to hear. "He should have come with all of you when we spoke of peace, and we would have given him the same quarters that you now have."

Little Eyes yet stared at the ground. His breathing became exercised.

Benjamin lowered his voice. "But I have no interest in revenge. That is not my custom." He extended his hand to Little Eyes, speaking now very softly, "And it is never too late to make friends."

Little Eyes lifted his eyes and stared at the open palm, then looked up and all around, first at his wife and children, then at the rest of his party, then at Peter and the other Sakonnets, and finally directly at Benjamin. He took a breath, calmed himself, and firmly took hold of the hand. He shook it.

All those around him grinned and wagged their heads in approval.

Returning to the others, they found an old canoe down by the water's edge. There, Benjamin appointed a Sakonnet named Lightfoot, Little Eyes' cousin and well-known friend of the English, to take Little Eyes and his company across to the island (Palmers Island) in the mouth of the inlet. "There you should wait until we return, so that you will be safe from the English, lest they find you and kill you and your little ones."

Little Eyes stepped up close to Benjamin. He bowed his head. "Thank you, Mister Church. Thank you."

Benjamin firmly rested his hand on the native's shoulder; he smiled. "We shall see you soon, on our return."

Then leaving Lightfoot with his orders, they continued their march to the south.

29

From there they turned southwest across the neck and toward Poneganset, heading to Russell's orchard so that they might have some apples for breakfast. Coming near the garrison, they dispersed into a thicket and spent the rest of the night without a fire, most of them falling back asleep.

When the morning light appeared, they approached the orchard and startled a small group of the enemy who had been sleeping there; who promptly fled. Then walking in among the trees, they saw that all the apples had been beaten down and carried away. They examined the ground and the dew on the grass, seeing the marks left behind; clues that told them that the enemy had slept there the night before, and that they were numerous. They had lain under the fences, and without any fires.

One of the English sentinels cried suddenly from the far end of the orchard, *"Captain Church! Come see this!"*

Benjamin ran toward the voice; Peter Awashonks came with him. Ahead they saw an open area at the edge of the fence, a wide piece of ground covered in blood. The sentinel who had called them was standing to the side, holding his nose and mouth.

213

Peter crouched and examined the ground; the grass was matted, the blood was spattered across the area in a geometric pattern yet with many small circles about a foot in diameter, circles where there was no blood. He looked up at Benjamin. "They used baskets." He dipped his fingers in the blood and raised them to his nose, rolling the blood between his fingertips and sniffing; he directed his eyes across at the fence astride the orchard; the gate there was open. "Swine," he concluded. He stood and faced Benjamin. "They kill all the swine; take the meat."

"An army has to eat." Benjamin nodded as he felt his grumbling stomach.

Peter looked all around. "They not gone for long."

Benjamin promptly assembled his men and departed, following the tracks as they led out of the orchard on the north side, toward Dartmouth.

Three miles later they came to a country road where the track divided in two; one veered left, to the west of the great cedar swamp; the other to the east.

Benjamin studied the path and then looked at Peter. "We should divide our men, follow both tracks. You take your Indians with you following one path; and I will go with the English following the other." Benjamin had seventy men in his company, half of them Indians, half English.

Peter shook his head. "No. We not go anywhere without you, Mister Church."

Benjamin stared at Peter, whose face was wrinkled now with worry.

"Not safe. English not know us. And now we cannot fight back against friends if they shoot us." He shook his head again. "We stay with you."

Benjamin turned and faced his most-trusted captain. "You have heard, just as I have heard, what some men said in Plymouth—not just about me, but about you."

"Yes. They no trust us."

"This will be a chance for us to prove ourselves, not just your men, but ours as well." He thought of another argument and pleaded from his heart. "This area has been abandoned by the English, and we know where Bradford's army is located. And it is not here."

Peter closed his eyes and thought a moment, yet shaking his head; unconvinced.

Benjamin placed his hand on Peter's shoulder. He spoke soft, but firm. "This is a short run. You will be fine. And we can show them how wrong they are about both of us."

After a long silence Peter sighed; he nodded. "Alright."

"Good." Benjamin smiled as he gave Peter's shoulder a good-natured shake. "Which way would you like to go?" He pointed at the path. "You decide."

Peter looked to the left, knowing that was the longer and harder of the two routes. "We are light, able to travel. We go west."

"Very well."

Agreeing that they would meet up that evening at the ruins of John Cook's house in Acushnet, they divided their group and each set off at a brisk pace.

Benjamin and his English soldiers followed the eastern track for about a half-mile as it veered into the heart of the swamp. There, he fanned out his men, a ploy he had learned from his Indian captains that had two key advantages: by spreading out, they appeared to be a much larger, more threatening force; and by not being together in a clump, as had been the tactic of the English, they were much harder to hit. He'd been told by Peter, "The English are as easy to hit as a house."

They were working their way along through the mire when Benjamin heard a whistle in the rear, which was the signal to halt. Looking back along his line of men he saw his brother-in-law, William Forbes coming toward him in a hurry (Forbes was married to his wife's younger sister, Elizabeth). Benjamin spun his horse around and hastened back to him, keeping as quiet as he could.

Forbes rode up close and whispered, "There's an abundance of Indians," he pointed, "They didn't see us. Come on back and see for yourself."

Benjamin followed him back to a small rise in the trail. They stopped there and peered to the west, far away through the trees, following the beams of the early morning sun as they penetrated through to a small clearing. He saw there a large band of natives, moving about. By their movements they were obviously unwise to their presence.

Forbes whispered, "It's mostly women. They appear to be gathering whortleberries (blueberries)."

Benjamin quickly passed his orders along the line. He appointed two men to ride with him, Jonathan Barnes and Jonathan Delano. Delano was familiar with the swamp and spoke the native language. The others were to wait to give them a head start and then ride out as fast as they could in a second wave.

Having good horses, Benjamin, Delano, and Barnes spurred their animals out of the scrub, riding at full speed toward the natives. In moments, they burst into the midst of the enemy: all of them women, unarmed; no men were in sight.

The women looked up in shock, dropped their baskets, turned, and took off running.

Benjamin and his men drew nearer, driving their horses after them in hot pursuit.

One of the women glanced back over her shoulder, looked directly at Benjamin, and came to an abrupt stop. She spun around and threw both arms up in the air, shouting, *"Church! Church! Church!"*

Benjamin recognized her instantly—she was an old Narragansett woman who had lived in Newport on the land of Peleg Sanford, a good friend. She had long owned a house and orchard there, but in the springtime, after the February and March reports of native attacks throughout the colonies, the distrusting English had driven her and her native neighbors out of their homes. Benjamin had become acquainted with her before she was forced to leave, and now, by sheer coincidence, his wife and sons were staying in her house, while he was away in battle. And amidst the chaos, screams, and gunfire that was happening all around them, he rode up close to her and yelled, *"Tell them not to run! We do not want to kill anyone! Please, tell them not to run!"*

The old woman turned and cried out to the others in her native tongue; Delano also called to them. A number responded immediately; they came to a halt and surrendered themselves to Delano and Barnes. But many others ignored the appeals and continued their flight, scampering away into the thickets.

Benjamin rode directly after them, easily catching up, then glanced past them. He saw more movement. Farther ahead, the men were running as fast as they could, leaping over the brush, ducking and darting between the trees, making their escape.

He kicked his horse and jolted ahead, flying past many, ahead to the very front of them. As he passed the lead runner, he leaned forward in the saddle and ripped the musket right out of his hand. He pulled to a halt and spun his horse around. He glared down at the native.

The Indian came to a stop, panting for air.

"You need to go back." Benjamin brandished the gun at him and then at the others to his left and right—more than a dozen warriors. "We are not going to hurt you."

They all stopped and lowered their hands to their sides. Those with weapons dropped them.

Benjamin looked all around him, expecting to see some others of his company there to aid him. There was no one. He had ridden out ahead of all his men. He was by himself, alone.

Realizing now the danger he was in, he seized the moment. Without hesitating, he took a firm grip on the gun and motioned with it firmly. He turned them about and marched them back over their tracks, back to where they had come from. Along the way, he spotted stragglers skulking under the bushes. He shouted brusquely at them, taking advantage of their fear.

They promptly complied.

Working his way back, he soon came across Delano, who was busily rounding up more prisoners of his own. The two smiled knowingly at each other and he felt the pounding of his heart begin to calm. The two men then rode together at the rear of all the captives they had gathered, some thirty Indians, as they made the long, slow walk back toward the place where they had started.

When they came near to that spot, he found his whole company was standing there together, guarding a group of prisoners, most of them women.

Forbes and a few of the others ran up to greet them.

Benjamin dismounted. He handed his reins to one of the men. "Take over these prisoners—put them with the others." He motioned quietly at Forbes. They stepped away from the others to speak in confidence.

Benjamin looked at his brother-in-law, befuddled. "Where *were* you?"

"We got bogged down in the swamp and had trouble getting through. And then we couldn't see or hear anything from you." Forbes was flush. "Benjamin. We heard gunfire.

We thought you must be dead. Then—then we *really* didn't know what to do."

Benjamin rubbed his forehead. "Well, I'm not dead. But I sure could have used some help. " He caught his breath, for he was still winded. "Without Delano, I might have been." He slowed himself and refocused, "Gunfire? *Who* was firing their guns? I never fired my weapon; neither did any of my captives. Tell me, was anyone injured?"

"No. None." Forbes stiffened. "But we did kill three of the enemy."

Benjamin took a deep breath and shook his head. He glared at Forbes.

"We had to, Benjamin. They were armed. They were going to kill us."

He placed his hand firmly on Forbes' shoulder, gritting his teeth. He thought a moment, sighed, but said nothing.

They assembled and counted the captives. There were sixty-three in all.

Then Benjamin took the old squaw out of the group for questioning. "What company do these Indians belong to?"

"Some Philip's, some Quinnapin, an' some wid Pumham."

Benjamin recognized the name of Philip's compatriot. They were Narragansetts, fierce fighters. "And are there others nearby?"

She nodded. "Abundance o' Indians. Dis swamp full o' Indians—from one end to da uddah. An' Philip an' Quinnapin, dey 'bout two miles dat way." She pointed west.

"Are there more of your people?"

"Dere were—uh, oh—near a hunderd men dat come wid us, and lef' us to gaddah whortlebaywies. Dey lef' fer Sconticut to kill caddle an' howses, an' to bwing back da meat. Dey comin' back soon."

Benjamin turned and looked to the east, in the direction of Sconticut, suddenly mindful of their exposure.

"If you go dat way, you will all be kil'd." She set her jaw; her mouth wrinkled up from a lack of teeth.

"Where did they cross the river?"

"Dey wen' stwait acwoss. Dat way." She pointed at the trail leading directly out of the swamp to the east, toward the upper crossing of the river, where it was wide and shallow.

Feeling now a sense of urgency, he promptly assembled his men and marched the prisoners out of the swamp, heading south, following the trail that ran astride the west bank of the river, directing them well away from the upper crossing. Several miles south, they made their crossing over to the eastern shore.

Finding a convenient place beside the river to secure the prisoners, Benjamin continued with Delano farther south to a place opposite the island where he had left Lightfoot with Little Eyes.

Recognizing them as they approached, Lightfoot paddled across to meet them on the eastern bank. He came quickly ashore and scurried up to them.

Benjamin briefed him on their exploits in the swamp and the intelligence he had received regarding the hundred Indians that had supposedly just gone down onto Sconticut Neck.

Lightfoot responded, "Yes. I watched them from the Island as they passed. I'll show you their tracks."

The three of them ran up from the shore onto the high ground and entered a meadow. Lightfoot directed their attention ahead to the trail, where the grass was beaten down, coming in from the left and continuing to the right, southward onto the neck. As they stood looking south, down onto the neck, they saw some distant movement. The same Indians were just then coming back.

Benjamin, Delano and Lightfoot darted back toward the shore and dropped down over the edge of the field. They kept low, watching and waiting.

The enemy approached single file, each of them carrying a load on their shoulder, a heavy piece of meat—a side of ribs, the large leg of a cow or horse. The first in line came through the meadow, halted, and set his load down. He stood there watching as the rest of them came up one at a time and also set down their loads. After a few minutes rest, they picked up their loads and continued to the north, following in their previous tracks, which was the shortest path back to the swamp.

Benjamin studied the warriors as they passed, thankful the Indians had not decided to veer off and take the path along the river. For if they had, they would have come across the tracks of Benjamin's army, and doubtless engaged them in battle, maybe even taken the lives of his men and freed the prisoners. He was thankful for the hand of Providence.

As soon as the last of the enemy had marched away and was out of sight, Benjamin sent Lightfoot in his canoe back to the island to fetch Little Eyes and the others; in the meantime he and Delano returned to the army. They arranged to meet Lightfoot later that afternoon in the meadow.

Promptly returning, Benjamin moved his men and all their prisoners up onto the plain, then south along the trail that had been left by the Indians. At the meadow, they gathered up Lightfoot, Little Eyes, and the others, then pushed east. As evening fell, they crossed over the Mattapoisett River. Benjamin decided they should stop there to rest, some four miles to the southeast of the ruins of Cook's house, well clear of that place, because so many of Philip's men were near to it in the swamp.

As they settled in, Benjamin dispatched Delano and two more of his men to go to Cook's house, their appointed place to meet up with the Sakonnets. The messengers found no one there, so they sat and waited.

Hours after midnight, Peter and his men arrived at Cook's house, bringing with them many prisoners. Then departing straight away toward Mattapoisett, they left to rejoin their English partners. Peter sent a scout ahead to let Benjamin know they were coming.

The rising sun was just clearing above the trees as Peter and his men rode in, proudly driving a long line of prisoners before them.

Benjamin was out in front standing, ready to greet them, smiling proudly as they rode into the camp. He tried to get a quick count on his fingers, but the prisoners were too numerous. He smiled up at Peter as he rode over. "How many?"

"Sixty-three," he said happily.

"Any of your men hurt?"

"No. But we kill'd some enemy."

"How many?"

"Three."

Benjamin shook himself. "Remarkable," he uttered.

Peter dismounted, his eyes narrowed. "What you mean?"

"Our numbers are exactly the same."

Peter stepped up close.

Each studied the other's face.

Then Benjamin reached forward, extending his hand. "We are clearly equals."

Peter smiled, took hold of Benjamin's hand and squeezed hard.

The others, both English and Indian closed in around them, rejoicing at the remarkable Providence that had guided their mutual success.

30

As soon as they had assembled all of the prisoners together, they set off to the east, crossing over the Sippican River and onto the road that led to Plymouth. Peter rode beside Benjamin at the front of the rest, so that they could share what they had separately learned. And despite having celebrated success, Peter wanted more. "We missed a brave opportunity."

Benjamin, who was always thinking ahead, looked across at his captain. "Go on."

"When we come upon great town of enemy, we see they belong to Captain Tyask, Philip's second in command. We fire at enemy before they discover us—ran at them with a shout. Then enemy men run, leave women and children, and many guns. We took Tyask's wife and son, others escape. But if *you* been with us, we could take them all."

"How many were there?"

"Hundreds."

"Hundreds?"

"Yes."

Benjamin tightened his grip on the reins; he shook his head.

"We better to stay together."

223

He looked across at Peter and nodded. "We should. We should stay together."

Arriving safely that afternoon with all of their prisoners in Plymouth, Benjamin sent a post to the governor in Marshfield, informing him of Philip's position in the great cedar swamp. Then he took a much-needed rest that night and all day Saturday.

On Sunday, July 30th, Winslow arrived in Plymouth before noon, having raised some men along the way. He summoned Benjamin to the meetinghouse.

Benjamin recounted his activity and assessment of the enemy's position and strength, answering all of Winslow's questions.

Satisfied with the fullness of Benjamin's report, Winslow interjected, "Based on the reports coming to me from the military leaders of the other colonies, they have made it too hot for the enemy, and now it seems the main force of them is down here, eastward of the Taunton River—confirming your words that Philip has returned to his old haunts. This gives you the opportunity, captain." He held a note in his hand.

Benjamin leaned forward.

"I received a post from Bridgewater, telling me that Philip intends to move to the north, across the river toward Taunton or Bridgewater, to attack those towns." He handed it to Benjamin.

Benjamin read it.

"I would like you to rally what men of yours that you can, along with the men that I raised, and to go out immediately in pursuit of Philip."

Benjamin handed back the note. He nodded and left with all haste.

Finding no bread in the storehouse, Benjamin was reduced to going door-to-door to gather up whatever household bread he could find from the local citizens. Then quickly assembling sixty men, more than half of them Indians, they set off in the early afternoon toward Bridgewater, swinging well north of the latest reported position of the enemy. They made it as far as Monponsett (Halifax) that night and stopped there to rest.

The next morning, Monday, they began their scouting ten miles to the south, along the upper skirts of the swamps above Middleborough. In the middle of the afternoon they heard a sharp exchange of gunfire at a distance and fanned out in search of the source. But unable to confirm the location, and considering that dusk would soon be upon them, they reassembled, veered back to the north, and camped in Bridgewater.

Before sunrise the next morning, having added another fifteen soldiers, Benjamin moved his company back to the south. Coming to the Taunton River, they discovered a large tree that had been felled from the far bank, making a bridge over the water. An Indian was seated on its stump, his back to them.

Benjamin raised his gun and stared down the barrel, studying the man: his long, feathered hair draped down the middle of his bare back, a back glistening in sweat from the heat of the morning; a glint of red was visible, his cape draped over his knee. The man sat still, obviously pondering something; with the sound of the water, he was completely unwise to their presence behind him. In these seconds of examination, seeing the cape, Benjamin imagined the Indian was someone of import, an enemy leader, a proponent of the carnage and destruction, but he could not be certain who it was. He tightened his feel on the trigger, concluding he should take the shot. He *was* the enemy. From that close distance he couldn't possibly miss.

225

But before he could pull the trigger, one of Benjamin's Indians yelled, reached out, and smartly shoved his muzzle down. *"He's one of ours!"*

Hearing the cry, the seated Indian spun around and looked directly at Benjamin.

Benjamin's warrior realized his error. *"That's Philip!"* he cried. The warrior raised his musket and fired.

But it was too late.

Philip threw himself off the stump, leaped down the bank to the river and made his escape along the sand.

Benjamin's men jolted up onto the tree and hastened over to the other side; he followed right after. Several veered off and ran in the direction of Philip, while the rest scattered in quest of the main body of Philip's army, which surely must be right there.

Bursting into their camp, the enemy was seen already dispersing into the woods.

Over the next few hours Benjamin's men were able to gather up a considerable number of prisoners: women and children, among them Philip's wife and son of about nine years old. Then questioning the captives and examining the tracks, they found that Quinnapin and his Narragansetts had been there and had drawn off to the west, back toward their home country.

Benjamin separated and interrogated the prisoners. "Where has Philip gone? Is he with the Narragansetts?"

But they all gave the same answer that Philip had "fled in a great fright at the first shot," and that none of them had any clue as to where he now was or where he was going next.

Benjamin left fifteen of his men there to secure the prisoners and to pick up any more they might find. With the rest of his men, he hastened after the tracks of the enemy, hoping to overtake them before the Narragansetts escaped over the river to the northwest.

They ran for several miles along the river until they came to the place where the Indians had crossed, then he and his company waded over through currents up to their armpits, holding their guns and powder up high. They emerged on the other side as wet from the river as they had been before from their sweat.

A mile farther, and still not having caught up with the enemy, Benjamin called everyone to a halt. He stood there winded, squinting up at the sun, shading his eyes. "We have to call it off for the day." He caught his breath. "We need to get back to the others before evening."

Several of Benjamin's Indian soldiers pressed through the others and up to the front of the line. Lightfoot spoke impassioned, "Let us continue. *We are so close.*"

Benjamin glanced again at the sun's position, then at his men.

Lightfoot continued, "The Narragansetts are *rogues.* They kill'd some of our relations. They kill'd Tockamona, Awashonks' brother, and others. We cannot let them escape our revenge."

The Sakonnets murmured and animated their support.

Benjamin studied their faces, reading their anxious thoughts; they were his best soldiers. He looked straight at Lightfoot. "Alright then. You should go. And I appoint you to be my captain, to command as many Sakonnets who want to go with you; and you should acquit yourselves like men."

Then shaking hands, Lightfoot and some twenty Indians left to continue after the tracks. Benjamin watched them scamper away like so many horses, strong and tireless. Then he turned and led the rest of his men as they worked their way back along the river.

31

Early in the morning, Lightfoot and his Indian soldiers returned to their camp, bringing with them thirteen new prisoners and a report of having killed several more. They were proud of the exploits, rejoicing that they had avenged themselves on the enemy. Then Benjamin assembled all of the prisoners they had caught the day before, together with Lightfoot's, and sent these along with a guard of a dozen men back to Bridgewater.

Now with the light of day, and no longer burdened with the captives, Benjamin sent out scouts to look for tracks, feeling more confident that Philip had escaped in a different direction from Quinnapin, and that he might yet be close by. A report came back soon enough of a track that led to a place where the enemy had built fires and roasted some animal flesh; but the fires had been put out and the enemy was gone. With this their only information, Benjamin assembled their army and they set out together to follow the track to the west, pushing along with haste.

Benjamin put his Indian soldiers out at the front, some of whom he had only recently captured and commissioned. He gave them orders to march softly, and if they were to hear any whistle in the rear, to sit down and wait for further

229

orders; or if they were to discover any of the enemy, to stop and wait for the others to come up. Benjamin intended to wait through the night and instead fall on them early in the morning, when they would all be sleeping and more likely to surrender without a fight.

As they continued in their hot pursuit, the Indians at the front came upon many women and children, and others who were faint and tired, unable to keep pace with the enemy as they fled. These new captives gave a report that Philip and a great number of his company were beyond there just a short ways. Benjamin's Indian soldiers told the new captives that they were prisoners, and if they would submit themselves, and be still, that no one would hurt them. And because the prisoners were hearing those words from their old acquaintances, they were eager to comply.

Shortly before sunset, there was a halt at the front. Benjamin ran forward to see why they had stopped.

Several of his men had gathered together, motioning for him to come close. They silently pointed ahead through the trees and whispered, *"Take a look."*

Peering over a rise in the trial, he could see the tail end of a column of the enemy, marching along, oblivious to their presence.

Benjamin leaned close and whispered to his men, "Dog after them. Watch their motion until it is dark."

A short time later, after the sun had set, Philip's army came to a halt and busied themselves with felling trees and chopping wood, making a great noise. And all the while that Philip's men were making their fires, Benjamin sent some of his men out, forming a ring around the enemy camp, sitting down in the dark swamp without any noise.

Benjamin crept around the perimeter, accompanied by several of his guards, assessing the enemy from all sides.

There, he saw his newest prisoners seated quietly between his native soldiers.

They looked up at him with great surprise and fear, for they had not previously seen there were any English soldiers among their captors.

Benjamin calmly whispered, "If you will be quiet and not make any noise or disturbance, you will be treated with civility." And seeing their doubt, he firmly added, "but if you will run and try to escape, then you will all be killed."

The prisoners saw his resolve. They held their silence.

Before the break of day, Benjamin had the prisoners assembled into an area away from the enemy camp, some twenty in all. He walked in among them with his guard of two men and Peter Awashonks to translate. He quietly addressed them, "I cannot afford any men to guard you now, as I and my men are about to set off on our fight. Now I want you to listen very carefully to what I have to say, for this is in your best interest." He paused and studied their expressions as they listened to Peter. He continued, "Afterwards, when the battle is over, or as soon as the firing has ceased, then you must come and follow after our army, and come to join us." He studied their expressions, then set his jaw as he continued; he pointed at his Indian guards. "You know that an Indian is as good as a bloodhound to follow a track. It will be in vain for you to be disobedient, or to try and gain anything by escape, for I and my men have taken many captives and killed many Indian rebels; and in little time, we will kill and take all the rest—and we will surely come and find you."

Benjamin understood that firmness was the best way to convince them of what they ought to do to save their own lives, and to restore peace. He silently studied every face, then nodded, turned, and walked away. He left them unguarded, alone in the swamp.

By this time, it began to be light. And as was his custom, Benjamin sent out two scouts to confirm the enemy's position and readiness.

But at the same time, Philip had sent out two men of his own to come back along their tracks, to see if they had been followed. On seeing Benjamin's scouts, Philip's men abruptly turned about and ran with all speed back into their camp.

Benjamin rose up from the thickets and ran after them in hot pursuit. Ahead, Philip's scouts were heard yelling and screaming the alarm, making the most hideous noise they could invent, and stirring everyone. The entire camp fled, left their kettles boiling and their meat roasting on spits. They ran toward the western end of the swamp.

Benjamin grabbed Isaac Howland and sent him with twenty English to sprint around the perimeter to the left, while he and Peter led the rest in a burst around to the right, planning to meet up together at the western end. He also left a dozen snipers in secure locations guarding the place where Philip had entered the swamp on the east, concluding Philip might reverse his course and try to escape along his own track.

Benjamin and Peter met up with Howland at the western end of the swamp. They spread out and stationed themselves, forty men, their weapons raised and aimed down into the swamp, primed and loaded, waiting for the enemy to emerge.

The large body of the enemy burst out of the swamp, well armed, headed directly at them. Then surprised, seeing the many English soldiers armed and ready to fight, they stopped in their tracks.

Peter yelled in their language, "If you fire one gun you will all be dead men!"

The natives looked left and right at Benjamin's men, counting the many guns at close distance, all pointed directly at them. They hesitated.

"We have you surrounded! If you surrender now, you shall have good quarters. We will not hurt you."

They stood still.

Without further hesitation, Benjamin and his Indians stepped forward between them and took the guns right out of their hands, guns that were charged and cocked.

They took some one hundred prisoners, mostly men, a few women and children. Benjamin's men directed them into a nearby valley, which was in the shape of a punchbowl, and there he placed a dozen of his men to guard them, each of them triple armed with guns they had just taken from the enemy.

Then Benjamin made his men ready for a fight, for he knew that the main force was yet to come up out of the swamp, and he still had not seen Philip, Tispaquin, Totoson, and several of the other prominent enemy leaders. And with the snipers trap he had laid at the other end, he knew they would be coming his way.

32

Benjamin ordered his men into the thickets to get out of sight, while he himself ducked behind a tree. He was sure Philip would be coming up from the swamp in their direction, following after the tracks of his own men—men that Benjamin had just taken captive. And as he waited, a hush fell over the swamp. He gripped his gun, feeling the blood pace through his fingers. In that silence, he came to realize that this next exchange would be different; these opponents were the hardened, committed warriors. This time there would be no easy, peaceful surrender. This time there would be blood.

When the tops of the enemy's heads first appeared, he waited, for he wanted their shots to be sure. They drew quite close; but before he could give the order, one of his men on the far right fired the first shot. This triggered the rest of Benjamin's men. The air exploded, from right to left, sweeping like a giant wave of fire and smoke, drawing a deadly semi-circle around the face of the enemy.

The enemy reacted unprepared. They unloaded all their weapons indiscriminately toward the cloud.

Immediately, Benjamin's Indians burst toward them through the thickets and out of the wall of smoke, screeching

235

and howling at the tops of the lungs. They leaped forward over bushes, rushing at them with their hatchets raised. The English followed.

Philip, with no time to think, recognized the ambush, and he had no taste for it. He turned about and ran. The rest of his company fled with him, straight back upon their tracks.

Benjamin took off, rushing through the brush. His plan was working. They were driving Philip through their camp and back out the eastern end of the swamp, the same path by which they had first entered, and straight into the sights of Benjamin's snipers.

When Philip's men emerged from the swamp to the east, they were met by a hail of bullets—Benjamin's sharpshooters were unloading one gun after another, for they were also triple-armed. A number of the enemy fell, and Philip stopped his flight, turned back once again into the heart of the swamp, having no choice now but to fight.

During the chaos and noise of the battle that ensued, Benjamin and his two guards ran into the fray and collided with three of the enemy. Two of them surprisingly surrendered without any fight. But the third was not about to yield to him. He was a great big man, stout and surly, with two locks of his hair tied up with red fabric securing a great rattlesnake skin that hung down the back of his head. Benjamin concluded he was Totoson, the murderous leader of the raid on Clark's Garrison. The Indian turned and ran.

Benjamin left the others and pursued him close. Then coming near to him, as he was running, he pointed the end of his gun between the man's shoulders and pulled the trigger. It misfired.

Hearing the snap of the lock, Totoson stopped and spun around. He raised his gun to Benjamin's face as he ran right at him. He squeezed the trigger.

Benjamin saw the open end of the muzzle and fell backwards to the ground.

But Totoson's gun also misfired. The big Indian dropped his gun and disappeared into the thickets, now joining the flight with his many fellows as they scattered.

Benjamin gathered his senses. He shoved himself to his feet and took off in pursuit, rushing ahead, bursting through the brush and into a stand of open trees. Looking around, getting his bearings, for there were numerous others fleeing all around, he spotted the fugitive now with a head start of some thirty yards. He doubled his speed, flying over the uneven ground, quickly closing the gap.

But the ground proved too uneven for his foe. The Indian caught his foot on a vine and tumbled forward, face first, hard onto the ground.

In a split-second, Benjamin was upon him, himself tumbling forward onto the enemy's back, with the barrel of his gun pointed forward like a spear. The muzzle slid up the Indian's spine and penetrated an inch-and-a-half into the back of his skull—an instant death.

Benjamin lay there a few seconds, seeing what he had done, and trying to catch his breath, observing the massive flow of blood, studying the dead man's head; he wondered, *Funny—Where is his snakeskin? Hey—Is this someone else?*

Glancing back over his soldier, he saw Totoson coming directly at him, scowling, screeching, flying through the air like a dragon, his arms stretched wide, with a hatchet in one hand and his knife in the other. And in that split second of flight, Benjamin heard the sound of muskets exploding and felt the wind of bullets flying past his head; he watched as Totoson took a bullet in one arm, veered off, and fled left into the thickets.

Benjamin staggered to his feet, winded. Then straightening up and looking back toward the swamp, he saw

Peter and several of his Sakonnets standing there, detaining their prisoners, smiling at him, having proudly fired the shots that probably saved his life.

By now the skirmish was over, the rest of the enemy fled. And as the clouds of smoke slowly lifted, his men came together, some of them herding a few more prisoners. Benjamin walked around and asked each of his captains for their reports. His first question to each was, "And what of Philip?"

One at a time he heard the same response.

"I don't know."

"I didn't see him."

And finally, "I saw as he escaped; along with his captains, and a number of his close men."

Benjamin hung his head in disappointment for he feared the cost of this engagement to his men had been great and knew that they had failed to end the conflict. But asking around, he heard that only one of his men had been killed, a Plymouth man named Thomas Lucas, whom he had stationed with the snipers. In the heat of the moment, Lucas had carelessly stepped forward from his secure position and taken several bullets. Benjamin felt the terrible weight of his loss. Losing even one of his men was one too many.

Then they counted the enemy casualties: there were thirty-three dead, and one hundred forty prisoners taken, including every single one of those they had caught the night before, as they had come to join them after the skirmish, just as they had been ordered.

And having no provisions, except for what they were able to take from the enemy camp, they hastened back to Bridgewater, sending an express in advance to prepare for them, for their company had become numerous.

There, the gentlemen and officials of Bridgewater expressed honor and gratitude and welcomed Benjamin and his men with great respect and kind treatment. Then Benjamin and his soldiers led their prisoners to the Bridgewater pound, where they were placed under guard, but also where they were given ample food and drink, which they took eagerly, for many had been near to starving from their year on the run. The sounds that came from the pound that night were the sounds of merry celebration, with the prisoners laughing together as loud as the soldiers; for Philip's Indians had not been so well treated for such a long time.

33

Peter, Lightfoot, and several other of Benjamin's native captains sat with Benjamin at a table, enjoying the evening that was now getting very late, leaning back with the comfort of a brew in one hand and a piece of meat in the other, stretching out their aches, feeling the slumber coming on, and willing at last to yield to it. For the first time in days they were not together riding on the edge of trouble. They were allowing themselves to relax.

Lightfoot leaned toward Benjamin, his smile changing to a serious expression. "Sir, you have now made Philip ready to die, for you have made him as poor and miserable as he used to make the English—for you have now killed or taken all his relations (his old Uncle Akkompin, who was killed while crossing the tree bridge; his wife, Wootonekanuske, and his only son); this war has at last broken his heart." He raised his mug and finished his thought, "—and now you shall soon have his head."

The other natives nodded. "Hear, hear," they all said as they raised their mugs toward Benjamin, then took a drink together.

Benjamin stared down at his mug as they celebrated, quietly examining his hands, recognizing how he had been

241

used to bring about the recent victories, the exploits toward restoring peace. But those exploits had been at a great cost, the cost of human blood, and so much of it spilt into the crimson sea of hatred. The thought of this cost made him feel sick. But seeing the current sentiment of his men, he could not, would not let his feelings rob them of their happiness. He concluded to himself, *I cannot change the past. No. I can only change the future.*

He looked up at them, studied their happy faces, and smiled. Then he raised his mug. "And *hear, hear* to you, my good friends. For none of the success I have seen would 'ere been possible without your dear service and sacrifice and the providence of God. Gentlemen. I thank God—and I drink to you." He put the mug to his mouth, drained it, and set it firmly on the table. "Now I think I shall find a place to lay my head." He got up from the table and walked away.

Awaking early the next morning, Friday, Benjamin gathered his men and moved all the prisoners to Plymouth, a full day's march. There, he learned that other successes had come upon the colony, particularly a report that Major John Talcot had arrived with his Connecticut forces at Taunton, having killed many Narragansetts as they fled to the west— perhaps the men that he and his company had chased in that direction.

In Plymouth, after receiving ample thanks from the local government officials, Benjamin's men disbanded; and he took the opportunity to return home to Marshfield, feeling much fatigued and ill of health from the heat and cold, and from wading for days and nights on end through rivers and swamps. He took with him a good number of his Indian soldiers, since they were far from their homes and in need of a place to rest; he was most happy to show them hospitality.

But it was not very long before he and his men were called to rally in Plymouth, as word had come that a number of the enemy had been discovered in Dartmouth woods. Nothing in the report suggested that Philip was among them, but Benjamin embraced the possibility that he might be. So on Monday, August 7th, after just two days' rest, he reassembled his company of Indians and added a few English volunteers—raising some fifty men in all.

Before the sun was much above the horizon, they left on horseback with all haste and few provisions, guided by their pilot toward the place in Dartmouth, a ride of thirty miles. They arrived in the late afternoon.

There, Benjamin scattered his men into groups and dispatched them to go out in different directions in search of the enemy, hoping they might be able to find Philip. In the evening, they reassembled in the appointed place, all with nothing to report, except Jabez Howland, his trusty lieutenant, who returned with his handful of men and a dozen prisoners. Then considering the lateness of the hour, and taking no time to rest, they turned back toward Plymouth, slowed to a walk on account of the prisoners.

Along the way, Benjamin questioned the captives. He found that they had been with Totoson, and had escaped from his most recent skirmish in the swamp. They said he should be able to find Totoson in a place not far from there, about "five miles west of Agawom" (which the English called Wareham). They gave more details and Peter said with confidence that he knew the location. Now finding this information useful, Benjamin dispatched twelve of his soldiers to take the prisoners to Plymouth, while he, Peter, and the rest veered hard to the east in search of Totoson.

Riding briskly through the rest of the night, they came at first light to Totoson's camp, directed there by the enemy's fires. Meeting no resistance, they captured the whole camp, except Totoson himself, who escaped with his eight-year-old son, and one old Wampanoag squaw. They disappeared together into the pines and ran off to the east toward Wareham.

Assembling the prisoners in the center of the camp, they recognized one old Indian as the notorious Sam Barrow, famous for his murderous attacks on English settlers, and who happened to also be the father of Totoson.

Benjamin looked across at the man. He understood his responsibility that came with his commission. There were rogues on whom he had no authority to show mercy, and he was to uphold the law. He also believed that execution was the proper means to punish a murderer of women and children.

He gathered several of his Indian captains and together approached the man, speaking loud enough for all his men and all the captives to hear. "Sam Barrow: the court has given you no quarter, on account of your murderous and barbaric acts. The sentence has already been handed out and has been shared with me and with other commanders. You are a convicted man. And seeing as I have been commissioned as an officer of the Colony, I must pronounce on you the sentence for your crimes; it is the sentence of death. And therefore, you are to prepare for it; for it will be delivered right now—before these witnesses."

Benjamin turned and studied the faces of the prisoners, waiting as his words were translated to them. He again addressed the condemned man. "Do you have anything to say before we carry out the sentence?"

Barrow looked at his captors with sad eyes. He nodded. "The sentence is just, and I am ashamed to live any longer." He looked at the people with him. "I desire no more favor, nothing more than to smoke a whiff of tobacco before I die."

Peter Awashonks stepped forward, pulled out his pipe and stuffed in some tobacco. He picked up a brand from the fire, lit the pipe and handed it to the native.

Barrow took the pipe, smiled at Peter and sat down. He studied the pipe in his hands, then raised it to his mouth and took a few whiffs. He closed his eyes to savor the smoke, then let it out in a great cloud. Smiling, he looked up at Benjamin and nodded. "I am ready."

Benjamin motioned with his eyes to one of his Indians who was standing directly behind Barrow; who promptly raised his hatchet and sank it unflinchingly hard into the condemned man's brains. It was an instant death.

Gathering the prisoners, they returned the rest of the way to Plymouth, arriving in the evening, exhausted from thirty-six hours on the road. Benjamin stayed at the home of a friend, intent on getting some rest.

The next morning, Benjamin was greeted by a post from Sandwich. He stood in the doorway, shaking the sleep out of his head, listening to the report.

The courier read the note: "An old Indian squaw came into town, sick with fever. She said she had escaped with Totoson and his son and had made it as far as Wareham. There, both he and the boy fell sick with fever. First the boy died, and a short time later, Totoson, beside himself with grief, died. Then the old squaw laid them down and covered their bodies with leaves; after which she set off to Sandwich and gave us her report. She offered to pilot us to the place of their remains, but before we could even prepare to go with her, she slumped to the ground and fell over dead."

As Benjamin listened, he stared down at the courier's dusty boots. Having heard the end of it, he looked up at him, thanked him, and watched the young man as he turned and walked away. Closing the door, he stepped back inside and returned to his bed.

34

Returning to bed after the sun was up was hardly effectual. Benjamin tossed about, trying to arrange himself into a comfortable position, longing to fall back asleep, seeking to rid himself of his exhaustion. Concluding there was too much light coming in through the windows, he pulled a sheet up over his head, then a blanket, anything to dull his senses so that he could return to slumber. But now feeling the heat of the covers, he flung them off. He lay there another minute, blinking up at the ceiling.

"That is *it*," he said out loud with disgust. "It is no use." He sat up, spun his feet over the edge of the bed, resting his hands on his knees. He gazed out through the open window, heard the birds singing in the trees, feeling the morning breeze sweep in. It was quite a lovely day. But being away from his family, he was in no wise able to enjoy it. He got up, washed his face, dressed himself and left for the meetinghouse.

Benjamin intended to speak with the governor. He asked about town and confirmed that Winslow was coming to Plymouth. Then he sat by, waiting for him with impatience.

Just before noon, Winslow approached on his horse, accompanied by his guard of five armed men and one of his servants. Winslow drew near to where Benjamin was standing by the hitching post. He smiled broadly down at him. "Captain Church!" he announced loudly. "I see you have once again brought us more success; and more prisoners." He pulled up, dismounted, tied the reins, and stepped around his horse. He extended his hand. "We owe you so much, Captain. So much."

Benjamin took his hand and gave it a firm shake. "Actually, sir. That is what I should like to speak with you about."

Winslow glanced quickly at his guard, then nodded. "Alright, then. Shall we go inside?" He waved toward the door to the meetinghouse. "But first, I could use a cup of tea, being rather thirsty from the road."

The two men went inside to a small chamber, the room that the governor used as an office. The governor excused himself and left, while Benjamin sat down in a wooden chair at the front of the desk. In a few minutes, the governor's servant came into the room carrying a silver tray with a pot of hot tea, fine china cups, and a small plate of biscuits. He set the tray on the table and left the room.

Benjamin was staring at the fine silver spoons when Winslow returned.

"Would you like some tea?" the governor asked as he walked behind his desk and sat down.

"No thank you, sir."

"Really. You should have some." Winslow picked up the pot and filled the two cups, then handed one across, smiling. "There is nothing better than English black tea."

"Thank you, sir." He reached forward and took the cup, raised it to his mouth and took a sip; it was only tepid, not hot. Then feeling impatient with the formalities, he set it down on the desk. "Sir, I have something to say."

Winslow took his sip, then followed with a quick gulp. He set his cup to the side and focused his eyes on Benjamin's. "I am listening."

"I have been in the war now for three months and I have not seen my wife and sons in all that time, but once for a few hours. And I have become rather weary and longing for them." He sighed, thought a moment, and straightened. "And I do hate to point this out, but feel I must, for you may not realize it—but I have had to equip myself and a number of my men out of my own provisions, my own powder, and even some of my own animals. I have paid people from my own funds, all for the benefit of the army." Again he sighed. "Sir, this war is costing me a great deal—financially and personally. I feel worn out. I need rest."

The governor leaned back in his chair and stroked his clean-shaven chin. "Yes, yes. I understand just how *much* you have given." He pushed his chair back, rose and stepped over to the window, looking out as he spoke. "And I can promise you that the government will make good on your service. We will redress your concerns and you shall have satisfaction." He turned back to Benjamin. "But we need you, Captain Church. We need you now more than ever."

"Indeed. I understand. But perhaps if I could just go to Rhode Island and spend some time with my family, then I would be of a better strength to return."

The governor turned and looked out the window, thinking to himself. At last he spoke. "I would like you to step over here and look outside."

Benjamin got up, stood beside Winslow, and looked out the window.

"Now tell me what you see?"

Outside, Benjamin could see a fine summer day. People were passing by on the street, some walking, some riding their horses, one man driving a wagon stacked with baskets of vegetables. Benjamin did not understand what he should be commenting on that was so unusual. He turned toward the governor with his brows raised. "What should I be seeing? There is nothing remarkable."

"So, would you say it looks like a rather ordinary day?"

"Yes, I suppose so."

Winslow placed his hand on Benjamin's shoulder and smiled. "Precisely, Captain. It is an *unremarkable* day, and all because of the *remarkable* efforts of your men, and of you. You have helped us to move once again toward peace."

Benjamin closed his eyes and nodded.

"Well then—" Winslow returned to his desk and sat down. "I am sure that you understand our predicament: that we need to take this war on 'like a business.'" He paused. "Now—did not one of my captains say that once?"

Benjamin faced the governor, recalling his own words, and the passion with which he had delivered them. The corner of his mouth curled into a grin. He nodded. "Yes. I believe I heard that once—from someone." He returned to his chair and sat down.

Winslow leaned across the table. "I really cannot afford to lose you, Captain. I would like you to at least remain on until we have taken Philip."

Benjamin set both hands on the table, staring at his teacup. At last he looked up and nodded. "Yes, sir. You can count on me."

"Good. Now let us talk about your next raid."

* * *

By Thursday evening, August 10th, Benjamin had gathered his Indian soldiers and raised an equal number of English volunteers to make up a company of thirty-eight men. Quickly assembling, they rode through the woods all night and arrived at Pocasset on Friday morning—a trip of fifty miles. There, Benjamin divided his men and went out in search of any recent tracks. In the mid-afternoon they reassembled at the east landing of Howland's Ferry, their point of rendezvous, hoping to share their findings.

The reports were not good; no one found any signs of enemy activity. Benjamin tried in vain to hide his disappointment from his men. He suggested, "Then let us ride the ferry over to Aquidneck. We can stop on the Island for the night to refresh ourselves and rest the horses." He intended to figure out what to do next after a night's sleep. He was simply too tired to think.

Now on the Island, Benjamin could no longer resist the draw of being so close to his family. He and half a dozen of his closest Indian soldiers rode south about eight miles to Sanford's estate, where his wife was then staying.

Alice was out in the garden when she heard the sound of the horses approach. She looked up and saw the riders getting closer, studying them, curious as to who they were. At last she recognized one was her husband. She lowered her basket, dropped it, and fainted onto the ground.

Benjamin dismounted and rushed over to her; he bent forward and tended to her, gently smoothing her hair out of her face, cupping her cheek with his hand, feeling its warmth. He studied her pretty face, remembering how much he loved her. He leaned close and embraced her, holding his rough, unshaven cheek against hers, and feeling her breath in his ear.

He raised back up, eyes fixed on hers as they blinked open. "Are you alright?"

She smiled up at him. "I am now." She pulled him close.

Then helping her to her feet, he began to explain his circumstance, and his plan to stay there for the evening.

But before Benjamin could finish speaking, Peter called out from over by the horses, *"Two riders approach!"*

Benjamin walked over to Peter and took a look for himself, seeing them coming fast, kicking up the dust. "By their riding, they come with tidings."

Coming close, they proved to be Major Sanford and Captain Golding; both men quickly dismounted.

"Peleg...Roger," said Benjamin as he shook their hands.

Golding tried to suppress a smile as he focused on Benjamin. "Would you like to hear some news of Philip?"

"*Yes*. Of course."

"We rode hard to overtake you—" Golding paused to catch his breath. "—There are just now tidings from Mount Hope. An Indian has come down from there, from Sandy Point, where he hailed across to Tripp's ferry, and they went and fetched him over to the Island here—and he gave me a report that he had just fled from Philip, who, he said, had killed his brother for giving some advice that displeased him, and he was afraid he was about to meet with the same fate."

Benjamin's eyes widened. "He was with Philip? *Where?*"

"On Mount Hope Neck. Philip is camping in a swamp on the neck."

Those words struck Benjamin like a bolt of lightning; his exhaustion fled. He knew exactly where that place was, not far at all. He glanced at Peter and his other Indians, then at Sanford and Golding. "Then we shall have the rogue's head by tomorrow morning."

Glancing back over his shoulder he saw Alice standing, clasping her hands together. He walked back over to her. "I—I have to go. I—I—"

She reached up and swept the tears out of her eyes, then put on a smile. She could not speak.

He pulled her close and whispered, "Pray for me."

She nodded.

Then he ran back over to the horses and the other men. Together they mounted, spun their animals around, set the spurs, and sped away in a cloud of dust.

35

It was evening when Benjamin and his company arrived at Tripp's Ferry. There, Golding and Sanford took Benjamin to meet with the deserter.

Before he could even be introduced, Benjamin recognized the Indian, "John Alderman," he said, smiling and extending his hand to him. "I have not seen you in a long time." He remembered the last time he had seen him, when he was taking some of Weetamoo's people over to Aquidneck for asylum. "Why did you go back to Philip?"

Alderman leaned back at the question. He shook his head. "There are some things you cannot explain, and some you regret."

Benjamin sighed. "Yes. So true."

Then Alderman continued and retold his story and circumstances of his flight from Philip. "And now you will find Philip on a little spot of upland in the south end of the Mount Hope Swamp, just at the foot of the mount."

Benjamin was familiar with the location.

"I can take you to him, to help kill him." Alderman glanced at Golding, then focused on Benjamin and intentionally repeated himself, "He killed my brother."

Benjamin considered himself a good judge of character, able to read a man's honesty. He had previously found Alderman to be trustworthy. He looked Alderman in the eye and made his decision. "Very well, then. You shall come with us."

Then looking across at Golding and Sanford. "And I would be fond of your company too—both of you—if you would join with us."

"Yes."

"Gladly."

By the time they got over the ferry and marched the two miles to the edge of the swamp, half the night was spent. The clouds glowed from the full moon above them, which gave them just enough light to guide their movements. Their greatest concern was the mist that hung in the air; it seemed like it would soon start to rain. It would be a challenge for them to keep their powder dry.

Benjamin called a halt to their march and assembled his company together. He leaned toward Golding. "I would give you the honor to lead the assault on Philip's camp."

Golding stared at Benjamin, feeling suddenly on the spot.

"All of my men I will give you are experienced in this. We have done this many times. You should not worry. You mainly have to be careful when you approach the enemy. Be absolutely quiet, and be sure not to show yourself, at least not until the daylight—we need to wait for the light so that we will not fire at our own men.

"And when you get near, you will need to creep along the ground on your belly, and get as close as you can. Then as soon as the enemy discovers you, just cry out loud. Your cries will be the word for the rest of us to fire and to fall upon the enemy. And when the enemy takes off from their upland and down into the swamp, then you shall pursue them with all speed, every man shouting and making all the noise you can. And we, lying in ambush, we shall immediately fire upon anyone who comes out silently."

He looked at Golding in the dim light. "Alright?"

"Understood."

"Good."

Then Benjamin counted out eleven men to go with Golding, including Alderman as his pilot. He sent them away.

After they had departed, Benjamin divided up the rest of his force into two groups of fourteen each, ordering that they go out in pairs, one Indian and one Englishman together, to protect his Indians from being shot by his own men. He placed Captain John Williams of Scituate in charge of the right wing of the ambush, while he took the others out on the left.

Having marched a distance into the swamp, seeming now farther than he had remembered, he stationed his men behind trees, each within sight of their own men to their left and right. He took Major Sanford by the hand and showed him the placements. Every man in his company had two guns. Benjamin whispered to him, "I have placed them so closely, it is scarcely possible that Philip can escape."

At that same moment, a shot whistled above their heads, followed by the distant clap of a gun. The sound came from somewhere in the center, toward Philip's camp. Benjamin suspected that someone had fired their gun by accident, for it was not quite light enough for the attack to begin. Before he could speak, a full volley followed.

In an instant, the enemy came rushing toward their positions. Benjamin's men around him were fast on the trigger to react; and the whole swamp exploded with the fire and echoes of their muskets.

On recognizing the ambush, the enemy spun about and fled in any direction they could. One surly old Indian cried out, *"Iootash! Iootash!"*

Benjamin yelled toward Peter, *"Who is that?"*

"Anawon. He telling his soldiers to stand and fight."

But the enemy soldiers paid no attention to their old captain. They kept on running.

All in a matter of minutes the enemy had fled, having found a gap in the ambush, rushing out of the swamp along the tracks that had been left by Benjamin's men. They all escaped unharmed. The swamp grew silent, fast.

Benjamin backed away from his men. He gripped his gun to his chest, trying to manage his emotions, emotions that just five minutes before had been floating in anticipation of victory. But in such a short instant, his well-laid plans had been utterly dashed. He looked up at the brightening sky and muttered, *"If only we had waited a few more minutes."* He slumped back against a tree and let his gun fall to the ground. He cupped his face in his hands, overcome by exhaustion—he had not slept in two days.

In the distance he heard a cry, "Captain Church! Captain Church!"

He looked up and saw Alderman running toward him through the trees.

Alderman came up excited and out of breath, "I shot him, sir—I killed *Philip.*"

Benjamin snapped alert. He felt his body shaking. He leaned close and whispered, "Tell me quietly."

Alderman caught his breath. "We were all in a ring around Philip's camp, and—and they were all sleeping— Captain Golding, he fired first for some reason; I do not know why—and then everyone in our group reacted, and unloaded their guns. Now, I was on the open side of Philip's shelter, standing beside Mister Cook. At the first shot,

Philip got up, threw his petunk (his pouch) and powder horn over his head, catched up his gun, and came running out of the shelter—directly at us. Mister Cook, he took dead aim, but both his guns misfired—and Philip ran right past us—and then Mister Cook told me to 'shoot!' And I shot him. I shot him *twice*."

Benjamin was now standing straight, reenergized. He smiled as he gripped Alderman's shoulder and squeezed hard. He leaned close. "Now let no man know this, not until we have driven the swamp clear."

Benjamin sent his men out in search of the enemy, scouring the swamp. But soon enough, the sun was up, the mist had lifted, and the dew was gone; so they could no longer track the enemy. Then declaring the swamp to be clear, he assembled everyone back into the middle of the camp.

Benjamin looked around at his men, seeing all of them weary, and reading their disappointment. "Gentlemen. I have some news for you. *Philip is dead*."

He watched as they jolted to attention.

"Alderman, here—" he placed his hand on the Indian's shoulder, "—*he* shot him."

The men erupted with joy, and the swamp rang out with shouts. *"Huzzah! Huzzah! Huzzah!"*

Benjamin turned to Alderman with a serious look. "Now take me to him."

They walked together past a small shelter where Philip had been sleeping, a shelter made of limbs, bark, and leaves standing at the edge of the upland. He stepped around to the front. The one open side faced down a small slope, leading directly into the swamp, built that way for a fast escape.

They descended the little rise and stepped down into the wet. The flash of rain that had fallen overnight had recharged the swamp.

"This way." Alderman pointed.

Benjamin and all his men followed.

"Over here."

Benjamin looked ahead. There lay the Indian, naked except for his breechclout and stockings, lying face down over his musket in the midst of the mud. There lay the great King Philip.

A hush fell over the swamp as Benjamin and his men approached. They crowded around and stood over him. They looked down, noting two bullet holes in the middle of his back, one of them through his heart. No man said a word.

After a moment, Benjamin broke the silence. "Let us pull him out of the mire and onto the upland."

Several of the Sakonnets reached down and grabbed the body by his feet and breeches and dragged him through the mud up onto dry land. There, they rolled him over and looked at his face. The Indians crowded around to see that it was him. The English, most of whom had never seen him before, just wanted to get a look at the notorious leader.

Benjamin stared down at the man that he and all his fellow soldiers had been chasing for more than a year—a man who had brought so much destruction on the English and native alike. He was now a pitiful sight, caked with mud, hardly appearing noble.

Benjamin thought a moment about what he should say, for he recognized he was standing at a significant moment, a sad moment. He stared down at Philip as the words tumbled from his lips. "Forasmuch as you have caused many an Englishman's body to be unburied, to rot above the ground, then none of your bones shall be buried."

Considering the practice of capital punishment exercised under his English monarch, Benjamin called one of the old

Sakonnets forward to be the executioner. He ordered him, "You shall behead and quarter the body."

The old Indian pressed forward through his fellow soldiers. He stood over the body with his hatchet in his hand. But before he began his work, he directed a speech to Philip. "You were a very great man. And you had made many a man afraid of you. But so *big* as you were, I shall now chop your *arse* for you." And immediately he went to work.

After the executioner had finished his job, he picked up the head and handed it toward Benjamin.

But Benjamin demurred. "No, give the head to Alderman. And—and give him also that remarkable hand." He pointed at Philip's right hand, which was famously scarred, the result of a splitting of his pistol. Everyone seeing it would recognize it was Philip's.

Then scouring the camp they found the remains of five other Indians they had shot during their attempt at escape.

Now having no other cause to remain, they returned to Aquidneck for several days of much-needed rest after which they ranged back through the woods all the way to Plymouth.

On their arrival, they were met with much acclaim and joined in with the festivities of a colonial day of thanksgiving. They also received their premium for every Indian they had killed: thirty shillings a head, which figured to just four shillings and six pence to each man. Benjamin considered the compensation to be paltry, but every one of his men felt that killing Philip was payment enough.

Alderman sold Philip's head for the same thirty shillings. The head was promptly taken up to the top of Burial Hill where it was placed onto a pike, there for all the citizens to come up and see.

But Alderman took the hand and kept it in a bucket of rum. He would show it to anyone who wanted to see it, a penny a peek; after which they would fondly congratulate him. It was a trophy for Alderman, a fine trophy of his conquest. And he got many a penny by it.

36

Philip was dead, but the war was hardly over. There were many pockets of native resistance that remained, causing no shortage of concern across the Confederated Colonies.

A post came from Rehoboth to Plymouth to inform the government that old Anawon, Philip's chief captain, had been ranging about the woods in Rehoboth and Swansea shooting English horses and cattle, no doubt for food. Benjamin had been at his home in Duxbury for nearly three weeks, resting, recuperating and visiting friends and relatives, and wondering if his service might now be over. But then a post came, summoning him to meet with Governor Winslow.

He reported to the meetinghouse in Plymouth before noon, shortly after Winslow had himself arrived. There he was directed into a meeting, where he was given a new charge, to go out after Anawon. Benjamin told the governor he would gladly go out again to serve the cause—he was never one to say no. But as he was walking away he expressed his true concern, "The encouragement in our last expedition was so poor, I doubt I shall be able to find enough men to accompany me."

Benjamin rode out in search of his former soldiers to join with him. First he traveled to the farm of Jabez Howland. Benjamin stood in the doorway to the barn and peered into the dark. When his eyes adjusted, he saw a man mucking out the stalls. "Jabez, you in here?"

Howland spun around, holding his pitchfork. "Captain!" He smiled at Benjamin and walked over. He glanced down at his own filthy, hands. "I would shake your hand, but well—you can see what I am doing."

Benjamin grinned.

"What brings you here?"

"Anawon has been spotted." Benjamin shared the intelligence. "I am raising a company to go with me on another expedition. I sure could use your help again, the help of my trusty lieutenant."

"Of course I will go." Howland jabbed his pitchfork into the pile. He stepped over close. "I will go with you captain, as long as there is yet one more enemy in the woods."

Despite the short notice, Benjamin was able to rally a number of his former solders: fifteen English and twenty Indians. They assembled together in Plymouth on Thursday and left right away. They ranged through the woods to Pocasset, arriving there on Saturday the 9th.

As they settled in for the night, Benjamin proposed that they travel the next morning over to Aquidneck to rest until Monday.

But the next morning, Sunday, a sentinel from the island arrived with an urgent report. "Early this morning, I was on the shore in Portsmouth, and spied a native canoe traveling from Prudence Island northward to Poppasquash Neck, carrying several Indians."

Benjamin's immediate thought was to race ahead to Mount Hope Neck, to surprise and capture those Indians, so that he could gain some intelligence from them concerning

Anawon's location. Then leaving in all haste, they crossed over to Aquidneck and rode on to Tripp's Ferry—they intended to take the ferry across to Sandy Point to possibly intercept the natives where the Poppasquash Neck connects to the mainland, north of Bristol. But the ferry was not running that day; a sign had been posted. Not to be deterred, Benjamin commandeered three canoes and began to ferry his men across.

Lightfoot came across in the second freight. When he landed, he saw Benjamin standing at the top of the strand, staring out at the wind and waves. Lightfoot and his men walked up toward Benjamin, pleading their concern, "The winds have become too much."

A great gust came up and almost swept Benjamin's hat away. He reached up to take hold of it while the gusts kept coming at his face. He nodded. "Yes. The crossing is impossible now. The rest of the men will have to come across tomorrow, on the ferry."

Benjamin counted the men he had with him; there were sixteen, all of them Indians. He addressed them, "I do not want to wait, to lose the chance to catch up with the enemy. Would any of you be willing to come with me up to Poppasquash?"

Lightfoot glanced at the faces of his men, seeing them nod, then turned to Benjamin. "We are sorry there are no more English with us. But yes, we will go." Then leaving their canoes high on the shore, they marched north, staying in the thickets, hoping to avoid being discovered.

When they arrived at the salt meadow north of Bristol Town, they heard a gun, seeming to come from the north; but they could not be certain. Benjamin called a halt until all of his men in the rear came up, then confirmed it was none of them who had fired.

Mindful of the small size of his force, Benjamin still thought it best to send a scout ahead. He leaned toward Lightfoot. "I would like you to search for the enemy; take three men with you."

Lightfoot nodded. "I will go; and I would like to take Nathaniel with me. He is well acquainted with the Mount Hope Neck, and he knows how to call them." The natives had a custom to call each other with a particular animal cry, like a wolf or loon, as a means to distinguish friend from foe. They would change the sound from time to time. Nathaniel was among those who had most recently been captured from Philip's men, so he would know the sound they used as their secret call.

Benjamin nodded. "Do not kill the enemy, but take them alive, that they might be questioned."

Taking Nathaniel and two others, Lightfoot crept on ahead.

Benjamin moved with the rest of his men a little farther, veering west toward Poppasquash. Again they heard a gun. It seemed to come from the same direction as the first, but farther off. Benjamin presumed that Lightfoot was already after that investigation, so he gave it no further thought.

They kept on going until they came to the narrow of the Poppasquash Neck, which was about one third of a mile in width. Here Benjamin stationed three men in the center of the neck to look out for any of the enemy coming out of the neck. He divided the rest into two groups of five each; he sent one group along the western shore of the neck, and he led the rest along the eastern shore; they were to meet up at the southern tip. Along the way, they looked for canoes and any tracks left by the enemy. Finding no signs anywhere, they headed back to the top of the neck, now feeling that their only hope lay with Lightfoot.

The sun was setting when they returned to the three they had left at the narrow of the neck. Those men told Benjamin that the scouts had not returned and "we have not heard or seen anything of them."

"Then we will wait."

An hour later, after it had become dark, Benjamin grew concerned as to what had become of his scouts.

Several of his men began to express their doubts that they would even return. One told him, "Maybe Nathaniel has met with his old Mount Hope friends and turned rogue."

Concluding they should make no fires for the night, and knowing they had no scrap of bread and nothing to cook regardless, they spread out and slept among the thickets, listening for a whistle from their scout, which was their signal. They spent a solitary and hungry night.

As soon as day broke on Monday, they drew off through the brush to a small hill for a view. There, they spied an Indian running toward them.

Benjamin ordered one of his men to step out and show himself.

The Indian ran directly up to him. He was Lightfoot.

Benjamin and his men popped up and gathered around him with great joy. "Do you have any news?"

"Yes—good news—" Lightfoot was still catching his breath. "—we are all well. We have caught ten of the enemy. We guarded them all night in the back room inside the old English fort."

Benjamin smiled. The fort that he had so strongly opposed was finally coming to some good use. "You can tell me more as we go there."

He and all the others began their march.

Lightfoot continued, "They are Anawon's men. They left their families in a swamp above Mattapoisett Neck and were down here hunting. Shortly after we left you, we heard another gun."

"We heard it too."

"It was in the direction of the old Indian burying place."

Benjamin knew the spot, two miles north of Bristol Town.

"We moved in that direction and discovered two of the enemy busily cutting up a horse. We ducked off into the brush on either side of the trail. Then Nathaniel told us he would call them, so he want back down the path a ways and began howling like a wolf, while we sat right there and waited. One of the enemy immediately left the horse and came running to see who was there, while Nathaniel continued his call, lowering his voice and drawing him along until he reached the spot where we jumped out and seized him. Then Nathaniel repeated his howling and the other left the horse and met with the same fate.

"We questioned the two men apart from one another and heard the same story. There were eight more who had come down onto the neck to get provisions. They had agreed to meet back together at the burying place last night.

"Now since the two captives were some of Nathaniel's old acquaintances, he was able to convince them. He told them he had a very brave captain, and how bravely he had lived since he had been with him, and how much they might better their own positions by turning to him. He told them they would find life better on the other side of the hedge.

"Then we waited a little while at the edge of the burying ground and saw the others coming. One at a time, Nathaniel howled them in; just as he had done with their mates before them."

When Benjamin and his Indians arrived at the fort, they were pleasantly surprised to meet there with Lieutenant Howland and all the rest of Benjamin's company. They had come across on the first ferry that morning and thought the garrison might be a good place to meet. They had brought over all their horses.

Being ravenous, they made up good fires and roasted up the horsemeat that their captives had taken. And though they had no bread, or any other morsel, each man had his own salt, which they always carried in their pockets, and used it to season their meat. To hungry soldiers, this made for a very acceptable meal. Benjamin and his men invited the prisoners to join with them in the feast. They were most grateful to be relieved from their miserable existence as fugitives; and several offered to continue the fight with Benjamin.

Their next move was to the place where their newest Indian soldiers had left their women and children, which was situated above the Mattapoisett Neck, just south of Swansea. There they surprised and captured all of them, together with a few more of Anawon's men who had just arrived. Upon examination, they all held to the same story, that "it is hard to tell where to find Anawon, because he never roosts twice in the same place."

One of the newest Indian soldiers, who went by the name Thomas, requested that he might be free to go and fetch his father, whom he said, "is about four miles to the north, in the Manwhague Swamp, with no one other than his young squaw."

Benjamin thought it would be a good opportunity to go with Thomas there, perhaps to gain some intelligence of Anawon. So he took with him four other of his Indian soldiers and Caleb Cook, the lone Englishman. He left the rest there and they all went off to look for Thomas's father.

When they arrived at the edge of the swamp, Benjamin sent Thomas ahead to see if he could find his father.

As soon as Thomas had left them, Benjamin's men discovered a track coming down out of the woods. He hid his men in the scrub to either side of the track and lay in hiding, to see who might come along. While they waited, they heard Thomas howling in the distance for his father, and then the sound of a response.

As they were listening, they thought they heard someone coming toward them. Peeking out, Benjamin saw an old Indian approaching with a gun resting on his shoulder. A young woman following close behind him, coming directly toward where they lay in hiding. Benjamin and his men allowed them to come up right between them, then jumped out and seized them both.

Benjamin separated them. He first questioned the woman, having one of his Indians translate. He warned her. "I will be able to tell if you do not tell me the truth."

She looked at him, visibly shaken.

"What company have you come from last?"

"Anawon's."

"How many were in the company when you left."

She thought a moment. "Fifty, or sixty."

"How many miles is it to this place?"

She shook her head. "I do not understand 'miles.' He is up in the Squannaconk Swamp."

Benjamin then questioned the old man, who turned out to have been a member of Philip's inner council; the young woman with him was his daughter. He gave the same exact account. Since Benjamin was unfamiliar with the location of the swamp, he asked, "Could we make it there tonight?"

The old man nodded. "If you travel with haste, you might get there by sunset."

Benjamin thought a moment. "And tell me, where were you going just now?"

"Anawon sent me down to look for some of our men who have gone down to Mount Hope Neck to kill provisions."

"Those men are now my prisoners. And we have their wives and children, too."

The old Indian looked away, then stared directly into Benjamin's eyes.

Benjamin heard someone approaching on the path. He looked back and saw Thomas coming along with his father and a young woman.

Armed with this incredible intelligence, Benjamin was faced with a problem. He knew that old Anawon was just a few hours from there, but he was in no good position to go after him. He had too few men; and now he was bogged down with new captives. And he would lose even one more of his men, having to send one back to his lieutenant to acquaint him with his situation. He called his men in close.

"I am of a mind to go after Anawon, as we know where to find him. Would any of you be willing to go with me?"

They looked at each other, then responded. "We are always ready to obey your commands."

He sensed their hesitancy. "But you have concerns?"

One at a time they reflected.

"Anawon is a great soldier, a valiant captain under Ousamequin, Philip's father; and he has been Philip's chieftain all this war."

"He is a very subtle man. It is said he would never agree to be taken alive by the English."

"And we know the men with him. They are some of Philip's chief soldiers. They will fight to the end."

"It is not practical for you to make an attempt with just a handful of men. It would be a pity if, after all the great things you have done, that you now throw away your life."

Benjamin felt the weight of their assessment. He studied their faces. They were good and faithful soldiers. He thought a moment before he responded, "I do not doubt that Anawon is a subtle and valiant man. But many of us have been searching for him for a long time, and without any success, and never, until now, could we find his quarters. And now I am very loathe to miss this opportunity—" he straightened tall "—and I have no doubt, if you will cheerfully go with me, that the same Almighty Providence who has thus far protected and befriended us, will do the same."

The men turned to one another, then to their captain. "Yes. We will go."

Benjamin looked at Caleb Cook, the lone Englishman with him, who had thus far said nothing. "And what do you think?"

Cook replied, "Sir, I am never afraid of going anywhere when you are with me."

Then Benjamin turned to the old Indian. "You know the way. Would I be able to take my horse with me?"

The old Indian shook his head. "It is impossible for any horse to pass those swamps."

Benjamin made his decision. He sent Thomas with his father, the man's squaw, and his horse back to his lieutenant with orders for him to move to Taunton with the prisoners. "I want you to secure them there, and then to come to the Rehoboth road in the morning, in which I might expect to meet the lieutenant—if I am yet alive."

37

Benjamin approached the old Indian where he was seated on the trunk of a fallen tree. "Would you pilot me to Anawon?"

The Indian looked up at Benjamin with tired eyes. "Sir, I give you my life, and I am now obliged to serve you." Then rising up, he led Benjamin and the others along the trail.

The old man stayed well out in front of them and they were hard-pressed to maintain his pace. He often looked back over his shoulder and when he saw that they were almost out of sight, way back in the trees, he would halt to allow them to catch up. They continued this way for nine miles through rough terrain: ranging through thick forest and scrub, stepping up and over rocks, branches, and fallen trees that lay strewn across the path.

Just as the sun was setting, the old man came to a stop and sat down. The rest of the company followed up behind him and sat as well, being weary from the trek.

Benjamin approached the old man and spoke softly. "What is the news?"

"About this time every evening, Anawon sends out scouts to see if the coast is clear. As soon as it begins to grow dark, they return." He looked at Benjamin. "We should wait."

273

Benjamin sat down.

"It won't be long."

When darkness approached, the old man pushed himself to his feet.

Benjamin stood up beside him and offered him back his gun. "Would you fight for me?"

The old man glanced down at the weapon, then bowed to Benjamin. "I will go along with you, and I will lay hands on any man that tries to hurt you. But do not ask such a thing." He grimaced. "Captain Anawon is my old friend."

Benjamin strained in the darkness to read the old man's eyes. He nodded his respect for him.

They moved out together, this time keeping close.

Soon they heard a noise echoing through the trees: a distant pounding, a steady beat over and over again, and then silence, and then the rhythm repeated. Benjamin took hold of the old man's arm. He whispered, "What is that sound?"

"It is the pounding of a mortar—grinding meal."

When they drew closer to the sound, Benjamin called everyone to a halt. He asked the old man for a description of Anawon's camp and the best way to get to him.

Hearing his report, Benjamin took two of his Indians with him, moving quietly, creeping closer to get a look, climbing up onto the top of an outcropping, inching to the edge to peer over. The source of the sound was just below.

From his high vantage, Benjamin looked down into the camp. He saw three small companies of Indians, not far apart from one another, well illumined by campfires. Directly below him, some forty feet down, he saw Anawon. He was seated in the opening of a shelter made by felling a tree against the rock cliff and stacking birch bushes against it. A young boy lay peacefully at his feet—Benjamin took him to be a son or grandson.

Benjamin's eyes ranged over the camp, seeing the fires burning, their pots and kettles boiling, meat roasting on spits. They were getting ready for supper. He saw the woman that was yet grinding cornmeal. He watched how she pounded a small stone against a hollow in one of the boulders, patiently feeding in the corn a few kernels at a time. Then scouting once more, he saw their arms; they were straight below him, all together in one place, standing on their ends against a tripod of notched sticks and covered by a mat to keep them from the wet or dew. Anawon's feet and the boy's head were almost touching the guns.

Benjamin leaned to his left and examined the trail that led down into the camp. It was just as the old man had described it. It ran along the sheer face of the rock like a staircase, steep and treacherous; they would have to lower themselves down by bushes and branches growing out from the cracks. Now satisfied with an understanding of the enemy's camp, he took his soldiers and crept back to where the others had been waiting.

He asked the old man, "Is there some other way possible to get into the camp?"

"No." The old man shook his head. "Everyone in the camp was ordered by Anawon to come in and out that one way. The swamp is all around them on the other sides. It would be difficult to come that way, and there is danger always of being shot."

Benjamin looked at his men, his small company. He glanced up at the stars. It was a beautiful evening. He made his decision. He explained to his men the layout of the camp, and how they would approach.

He looked at the old man. "You will go down first with your basket on your back. I will follow in your shadow. And then your daughter shall come after me." Benjamin intended that if Anawon saw them coming down, he would think nothing of it.

Then hearing the echoes of the Indian woman's mortar as it persisted and pounded through the trees, he spoke to everyone, "We shall walk only to the beat of the mortar; and stop when it stops. Its sound shall conceal our footfalls."

They all moved together to the top of the outcropping and silently began their descent by the rocky staircase. Benjamin crept close behind the old man, gripping his hatchet in his hand.

At the foot of the climb, Benjamin stepped smartly over the head of the young boy, directly to the guns. The boy looked up and saw him, threw his blanket over his head, and shrunk into a heap.

Anawon started up from his seat and cried out, "Howoh!" But seeing he could not escape, he fell back and lay silent while Benjamin secured the guns.

Benjamin's men came quickly in after him. He whispered his orders to his Indians to rush through to the other fires, to the other companies, and told them quickly what to say, lines they themselves had heard and spoken before.

His men ran into the midst of the three camps, brandishing their guns. They blurted out the message. "*Anawon is taken!*" Then seeing the men fall back, they continued their speeches. "It is best for you to quietly and peaceably surrender yourselves. For if you pretend to resist or try to escape, it will be in vain, for none other than Captain Church, and his great army have entrapped you; and they will cut you all to pieces!" Then they continued, "If you submit yourselves and deliver up your arms, and stay right where you are until the day, then we assure you that our captain, who has been so kind to us, he will also be kind to you."

Seeing that Benjamin's soldiers were their old acquaintances, and some of them even relatives, they readily complied, handing over their pistols, hatchets, and knives. One of Benjamin's soldiers stayed as a guard in each camp, while the others gathered up the weapons and carried them back to Benjamin.

Since the danger of the moment seemed now to have been settled, Benjamin turned to Anawon. "What do you have for supper? For I have come to sup with you."

"Taubut," said Anawon in his very big voice—he was a tall, imposing figure of a man. He turned and gave instructions to his women in his native tongue, and they busied themselves with the preparations.

Anawon turned back to his captor. "Cow-beef, or horse-beef?"

Benjamin was surprised by Anawon's English. But then he figured the old man must have learned a few English words in his long life. He smiled. "Cow-beef would be most acceptable."

The supper was soon ready. The old squaw he had seen with the mortar presented him with a bowl of steaming beef and a side of hot corn meal. He reached into his pocket and pulled out his little bag of salt, the only provision he had with him. He seasoned the beef. It was a hearty and delicious meal indeed.

After supper, Benjamin addressed two of his men. Anawon was right there, but Benjamin was not at all concerned that the old Indian would be able to listen to what he was about to say, since he presumed Anawon did not know English. "I want you to go to the other companies to tell them that 'Captain Church has killed Philip,' that I have taken their friends in the Mount Hope Neck, but have spared all their lives, and that I suppose now that all of the enemy has been subdued. Then I want you to tell them that if they will be orderly, stay in their places until the morning, then they shall each of them again live free, except for Anawon, for I must take him with me to Plymouth to plead for his life, and there his fate will be decided by my masters." He glanced across at Anawon, who sat stone-faced. "It is not in my power to promise him his life." He turned back to them. "Then tell them that in the morning we intend to take them all to Taunton where they will be reunited with their friends. Those are my terms."

His men left.

They returned a short time later with happy expressions. "All of Anawon's company has yielded to your proposals."

Benjamin took a deep breath. He nodded at them. Then feeling himself suddenly taken with exhaustion, for he had been two days and one night without sleep, he appealed to them, "Let me sleep for two hours; then you can sleep for the rest of the night." He lay down on the ground and adjusted himself, trying to find a comfortable position so that he might fall asleep.

The camp soon fell quiet and the sounds of the swamp took over the night.

After a little while, strangely unable to sleep, Benjamin sat up. He saw that both of his guards had fallen asleep. He stared across at Anawon.

Anawon stared back, both eyes open. It was apparent that he and the old Indian were the only ones in camp not sleeping.

They looked at each other for an hour in total silence.

Abruptly, the old Indian stood up and set his blanket aside. The only clothing he was wearing were his small breeches. He stepped out of the shelter and walked away, through the middle of the camp and toward the swamp.

Benjamin wondered where Anawon was off to. He tried not to be concerned. *He has just gone off to ease himself—*

278

far enough to have privacy, and not offend anyone. He leaned back against a stone, figuring the old Indian would return in a minute.

One minute turned to two, then to five, then ten. Anawon had not yet returned. Benjamin looked at the pile of guns, hatchets, and knives. He had all of Anawon's arsenal right there beside him. *No. Wait. Maybe they have other weapons hidden in the swamp.*

He crawled over close to the guns and sat up next to the boy, figuring if Anawon had gotten himself a gun, he would not risk shooting the youth, probably his own son.

At a distance he heard someone coming, from the same direction in which Anawon had left. The full moon was now directly overhead, shining brightly across the camp. As he kept looking, he saw Anawon approach, the light falling on the top of his head and shoulders and onto something large that he held before him in his hands. He was carrying some sort of pack.

Anawon stepped into the shelter; he dropped down to his knees directly in front of Benjamin, offering him what he held in his hands. He astonished Benjamin as he spoke to him in plain English. "Great captain, you have killed Philip and conquered his country; for I believe that I and my company are now the last that war against the English; so I suppose the war is ended by your means; and therefore these things belong to you."

Benjamin recognized there was a lot more to this old Indian than he had presumed. He watched in silence as Anawon opened the pack.

The old Indian pulled out Philip's belt. It was nine inches wide and some five feet long, hand woven of black and white wampum beads, with figures and flowers, birds and beasts, stunning in its beauty, shimmering in the moonlight. He pulled out a second belt, much narrower than the first, but made in the same manner. "This is Philip's crown." Anawon held it up to his forehead to show how it was to be worn. Two flags hung from it, to go down the back of his head, with a neckpiece of silver with a star of gold that hung down in front of his chest. Both of the belts were edged with red hair, which Anawon said, "We got from the Mohawk's country." At the last, Anawon pulled out two horns of glazed powder and a red blanket. "These are all of Philip's royalties, with which he would adorn himself whenever he sat in state." He smiled at Benjamin and handed the objects to him.

Benjamin took them in his hands, stared at them, feeling their weight and the magnitude of the moment. He looked up at Anawon and nodded his respect.

The rest of the night, Benjamin and Anawon sat together in discourse. Anawon spoke proudly of his past, years ago, and his many years in war against the other Indian nations when he served Ousamequin, Philip's father. Benjamin delighted at the stories, which he presumed no Englishman had ever heard.

In the morning, as soon as it was light, Benjamin and his men marched with their prisoners up out of the swamp country toward Taunton. Some four miles outside the town, they met with his lieutenant and his company. All of them expressed great joy and surprise in seeing them and their great company of prisoners, "more than we ever expected." After this they marched together into Taunton, arriving there to much acclaim and kind treatment. Benjamin was grateful most of all to be able to spend the night catching up on his sleep.

The next morning, Wednesday the 13th, Benjamin took Anawon and a half-dozen of his Indian soldiers with him to Aquidneck, sending the rest back with his lieutenant to Plymouth. And after spending a couple days on the Island,

Benjamin departed with his wife, Alice, and their two young sons, to take Anawon to Plymouth.

38

Benjamin had been in Duxbury a week when he was summoned again to Plymouth to go out after yet another band of Indians who had been haunting the woods between Plymouth and Sippican, damaging property of the English, killing their cattle, horses, and swine.

He assembled two-dozen men and went out in the afternoon in pursuit, traveling some six miles to the south. The next morning, Tuesday, they discovered a track and followed it for the whole of the day. When the afternoon grew late, Benjamin sent two of his Indians ahead to see what they could discover, while the rest of them followed slowly.

Shortly after the sun had set, while the sky was yet glowing in the west, the scouts returned with a report that they had spotted the enemy ahead a short ways, in a place where the brush was thick. The enemy had set up camp for the night there and were reclining around their fires.

Benjamin ordered his men to creep as close as they could until they should be discovered, and then to rush in and take them alive, if possible, for the prisoners were their pay. Then working their way to the edge of the camp, they all ran in together yelling and brandishing their hatchets. This caught the enemy completely off guard, and before they could even rise to resist, the natives were all taken captive; not one of them escaped. There were fifteen in all, including women and children.

When Benjamin examined them, he determined that they belonged to Tispaquin's company (Assawompsets), and that among the captives was Tispaquin's wife, Amie, Philip's sister. All those he questioned gave the same account, that Tispaquin and two other men had gone south to Agawom and Sippican to kill horses. They were not expected to return for two or three days.

On hearing Tispaquin was their leader, Benjamin reflected on the man, for he was a warrior of renown, the "Black Sachem," fierce in his fighting and gifted with an uncanny ability to survive. Many Indians had elevated him to legendary status, even saying that "Tispaquin is such a great powwow (wizard), that no bullet can enter him." But Benjamin was not to be swayed by legend. Still, he had an immediate thought that he might try to enlist that great captain to help the Colonies in the war that had just broken out with the Abenakis.

But having no mind at present to sit there and wait for him for two or three days, Benjamin selected two old squaws out from the prisoners. He told them, "I am going to leave you here. When Tispaquin returns, you shall tell him 'Captain Church has taken his wife and children, and the rest of the company; that I will spare all their lives, and his too, if he and his other two men with him will come to Plymouth and agree to be one of my soldiers to fight with me against the eastern Indians.'"

Seeing they were agreeable to his plan, he left them there well-provided-for, and with biscuit enough for Tispaquin. Then he gathered up the rest of the captives and took them back to Plymouth, feeling good about his plan, confident that Tispaquin would comply and turn himself in.

Two days later, on Saturday, Benjamin departed for Boston to meet with the commissioners of the Confederated Colonies who were then sitting, so that he could discuss his plan for how he might help them prosecute the war in the east. After several days of face-to-face meetings, finding them less than anxious to embrace his plan, he returned to Plymouth.

When Benjamin rode back into the center of town the following Wednesday, he saw ahead the familiar figure of Jabez Howland on his mount, riding toward him. Howland saw him coming, pulled back on the reins and stopped. He sat back and waited for Benjamin to come close.

Benjamin pulled up beside him. "How is my lieutenant today?"

Howland looked down at his hands. "I don't suppose you have heard?"

"Heard what?"

Howland shifted his wait in the saddle.

Benjamin could read in Howland's eyes that he had something hard to say.

"Tispaquin turned himself in—the day you left for Boston."

Benjamin brightened, suddenly believing that Howland had been trying to take him off guard, to play a joke on him. It was a pretty fair try to get even for the joke he had played on Howland. "You really had me fooled." He smiled. "That is wonderful."

Howland turned stern. He shook his head. "No, Benjamin. No, it is not."

Benjamin's smile quickly faded. His eyes widened. "Alright. Tell me."

Howland could not look him in the eye. "The council was none too attracted to your idea, to use Tispaquin in our army—" He raised his hand to his mouth. "—the thought of it makes me sick." He turned away.

Benjamin leaned close, now anxious for the full report.

"Someone got the idea to see if the legend about Tispaquin was true—"

He winced.

"—they shot him, Ben. They shot him."

Benjamin recoiled. His face turned white.

"And that is not all that they did while you were away." Howland pointed up to the top of burial hill. "They cut off his head and put it up there on a pike—"

Benjamin snapped his head around to look.

"—they put it right up there next to Philip's—*and Anawon's.*"

Benjamin gasped. He stared at the top of the hill, seeing now the array of pikes, side by side, and atop each one, a grizzly, rotting head.

Benjamin hung his head and fumed. He tightened his fists and felt the whole of his body shake.

39

The leaves had fallen and the trees were bare when Benjamin received the notice that he was to come to Plymouth to appear before the general court. He had long since exhausted his emotions and turned away many a friend with his anger over how the hundreds of prisoners he had taken had been abused, killed, and sold into slavery. By now he had become numb to the thought he had once held, the thought that he could convince the government that they had nothing to fear from the Indians, who wanted only to return to their lands and live as peaceful neighbors. But for the politicians there had been too many English killed in the war, too much property destroyed, for them to ever again extend a friendly hand to the natives. The political elite had yielded themselves to the voice of the times and chosen to appear sympathetic to the hatred of their citizens. Too many of the people wanted revenge; and too few understood the need for grace. As a result, Benjamin sensed that life between the English and the Indians could never be like it had been in the days of their fathers. There was no more point in his arguing to go back to those days. He understood now that his opinion did not matter. Worse than that, he began to

287

understand that he had been used to promote a change that he had never intended.

When Benjamin arrived at the meetinghouse, he was not at all sure what he would be hearing, nor did he have any words planned to say. All he had in mind was the likely purpose of the court, which was to recognize his service to the colony, a bit of praise he would not have sought, but which he would be graceful enough to accept. But considering how much he had given of his personal wealth to fund and supply his service and that of his men, considering all this, he hoped deep-down that they would offer at least to reimburse his expenses. That would be proper recognition for his service.

When Benjamin stepped over the threshold and into the meeting, he looked ahead to the front of the room and saw there the officials seated at the table. They were engaged in some sort of discussion. He stood awkwardly in the doorway.

Governor Winslow had been in the middle of making some point when he noticed Benjamin step in. He interrupted himself, turned to the audience, and raised his voice. "...We shall table this matter in favor of one far more important. For our guest of honor is here." He rose to his feet and extended his hand toward the doorway. "Captain Church has just arrived." He smiled broadly and began to clap his hands.

The audience spun their heads around. They promptly rose to their feet, along with the rest of the men in the council. The room erupted in applause and shouts. *"Hear! Hear!"* The windows shook from the sound.

Benjamin removed his hat, and bowed with a graceful flair. He smiled broadly.

Winslow waved toward Benjamin, imploring him to come forward.

The applause continued as he stepped to the front of the room.

Winslow directed him to the empty chair to the right of the table. Then as the applause subsided, the men at the front sat down. The audience quieted and sat, as did Benjamin.

Winslow shuffled through the papers before him and pulled out the one he wanted. He held it up as he addressed everyone. "I have here a resolution." He read it aloud:

"Be it resolved:
THE GENERAL COURT OF THE COLONY
OF PLYMOUTH as a body does hereby recognize
CAPTAIN BENJAMIN CHURCH for his service
to the colony during the war, how through his
singular acts of courage he did lead his company into
battle, how he brought victory over Philip, the late
sachem of Mount Hope, our mortal enemy, and over
many of Philip's allies that lurked about in the
woods, who had brought death and destruction upon
our plantations and villages, and disturbed the peace
of his Majesty's subjects by their frequent robberies
and other insolences. And insofar as Captain
Benjamin Church raised and led a company of
volunteers under the providence of GOD and with
the great success of his intelligence, he discovered,
pursued, fought with, destroyed and subdued our
Indian enemies, helping to bring the murderous
rogues to their just end, and likewise bringing their
fellow actors, those complicit to the heinous
villainies, to bring those to us as prisoners, to be sold
as perpetual slaves, and taking all their possessions as
plunder, as retribution for their acts of war; and so it
is with the full and complete measure of our

*gratitude that we do now thank CAPTAIN
BENJAMIN CHURCH for his faithful service to
GOD, his Majesty's interest, and the interests of the
Colony.*

Benjamin had stared silently at the floor as the
document was read. He kept waiting for the part—the part
about the reimbursement for the great cost of his service—
the part that was never read. He kept staring at the floor.

Winslow turned to the other leaders seated beside him.
"Do I hear a motion to approve this resolution?"

"So moved!" shouted one of the men.

"And a second?"

"Second!"

"Any discussion?"

The men at the front held silent as Benjamin kept
staring at the floor.

"All those in favor, say 'aye.'"

"Aye!"

"Opposed?"

Silence.

"Then the resolution is approved." Winslow dipped his
pen in the well and made his final markings on the
document.

Winslow rose to his feet, stepped over toward Benjamin,
and extended his hand. "Captain Church."

Benjamin rose to his feet and took the governor's hand.
He looked Winslow in the eye and smiled politely as he
shook it.

Winslow turned to the audience and lifted his hands as
he began to applaud. The audience rose in one accord again
and joined with him.

Benjamin tilted his head toward everyone and smiled.
Then he put his hat on and walked out of the meetinghouse,

while they remained standing and clapping. And as he walked away, he heard the applause fade, followed by the sound of the gavel.

The court had resumed its other business.

And all he had received was their thanks.

40

In January of 1677, Benjamin had received yet one more
commission from Governor Winslow to raise an army and
lead them out against the Indians that yet remained in the
woods, wrecking destruction and stealing English property.
Benjamin could not condone such criminal acts, nor could
he deny his obligations as a member of the militia, thus he
had agreed to serve, doing so with the hope that his presence
in the field would help to bring about non-violent surrender
of the criminals and the restoration of peace. After several
weeks in the field, he had returned with a handful of
captives, but instead showed his mercy on them by restoring
them to their homes; refusing to make any of them slaves.
Feeling that the war was principally over, he and his men
had returned to their homes.

Yet for the next year, the war had continued in the east.
And through negotiations between the military leaders of
Massachusetts and the sachem leaders of the Abenaki, the
Treaty of Casco was at long last signed on April 12th, 1678,
bringing an official end to King Philip's War.

Now, a year later, John Leverett, the governor of
Massachusetts, summoned Benjamin to meet with him in

Boston on "some matter of importance regarding the conclusion of the hostilities."

Arriving at Leverett's home, Benjamin was ushered inside by one of the servants, who told him that the governor lay sick.

"Perhaps I should return another time."

"No." said the servant, "The governor was most insistent that I take you in to meet with him." He guided Benjamin to the governor's bedchamber.

"Captain Church, I presume," said Leverett as he sat in bed, "Do come in."

Benjamin removed his hat and bowed. "Yes, your glory."

Leverett pointed. "Bring that chair over here and sit beside me."

Benjamin obliged.

"I have been anxious to have you come here and to give me your account of the war, for inasmuch as I understand you have been present at such events that were of singular importance in its resolution and conclusion—events I would be most pleased to understand in some detail."

Benjamin nodded. "I am happy to tell you what I have seen with my own eyes."

For the next two hours, he gave an account of many of the events of the war, even expressing some of his deepest concerns about how the natives that surrendered had been ill-treated, and how little the government had compensated those who had so eagerly served in its defense.

Leverett remained engaged, often interrupting and asking questions, and not the least offended by Benjamin's concerns.

At length Benjamin concluded.

The governor reached across and took hold of Benjamin's hand. "My dear captain, I find myself troubled over how poorly your government has behaved in consideration of all you have done for it, and the brunt you have born. I promise you now, if it pleases God that I should live, I promise that I shall raise for you a brace of one hundred pounds from the Massachusetts colony, and I shall endeavor that the rest of the colonies shall proportionately do the same."

Benjamin felt his heart swell with hope, hope he would at last be properly thanked for his service. He firmly shook the governor's hand and thanked him. "I am sure that God is in control of all matters."

Benjamin bowed, bid the governor farewell, and returned to his home in Little Compton, for that was where he then resided.

Three weeks later, Benjamin was over on Rhode Island for business. On a Friday night he was in the local tavern, seated at the table with several friends. He had just finished his brew and was thinking it was time to leave when Roger Golding stepped in.

Golding saw Benjamin and came directly over to the table.

Benjamin pointed to the empty chair, smiling. "Come and sit with us."

Golding stood behind the chair. "Benjamin, I just heard the news." He wore a serious expression.

Benjamin stared up at him.

"Governor Leverett—"

Benjamin leaned forward. "Yes."

"—the governor is dead."

Benjamin sank back into his chair and stared at the table. He took a deep breath and looked up at Golding. "Thanks, Roger. Thank you telling me." Benjamin sighed as he pushed himself to his feet. "Here, have a seat." He picked up his empty mug and turned to his friends. "I am going to have another. Can I get you all one?"

They looked up at him and nodded.

* * *

Other than a few pounds for the prisoners he had brought in, Benjamin Church never received payment from the Confederated Colonies for his service in the war.

91532957R00177

Made in the USA
Middletown, DE
30 September 2018